Frogs and Snails and Old Dog's Tales

Books by this Author:

Man in the Middle
Frogs and Snails and Puppy Dog's Tales
Frogs and Snails and Big Dog's Tales

Frogs and Snails and Old Dog's Tales

Short Stories from Ireland

A Children's Book for Adults

By
Frank Murney

Order this book online at www.trafford.com
or email orders@trafford.com

Most Trafford titles are also available at major online book retailers.

Printed in the United States of America.

ISBN: 978-1-4269-6484-8 (sc)
ISBN: 978-1-4269-6485-5 (hc)
ISBN: 978-1-4269-6486-2 (e)

Library of Congress Control Number: 2011906120

Trafford rev. 07/13/2011

www.trafford.com

North America & International
toll-free: 1 888 232 4444 (USA & Canada)
phone: 250 383 6864 ♦ fax: 812 355 4082

Red Morgan, Po Hillen, and the gang are reaching the end of their school days. The now infamous class of 3C is about to be released on an unsuspecting world. They may be older, but their exploits continue to be as crazy as ever in the 1960s and 1970s.

In this third book in the series, Anto Falsoni continues to act as the bookie for the many schemes the gang dreams up—and somehow always comes out on the winning side. After interviews during the school year, most of the gang is recruited to complete a three-month course in Dublin with a company intending to open a factory in Newry. Living together in the big city leads to many hilarious situations both at work and at home. Their adventures, if anything, rival their school days.

It was just a short time ago when the boys would only talk about football; now the conversation has turned to plans of purchasing engagement rings.
Even at this stage of their lives, the banter and teasing never stops as they move through life at a breathtaking pace that embraced chaos with what appeared to be a natural ethos.

Dedicated to the memory of

Nelly and Padge

Special thanks to

Sharon Oseas
Hazel Abdulla
Joyce Harvey

*For their generosity of time,
encouragement
and talent.*

Characters

Due to the fact that the same characters appear in almost all the stories within, I hope it may be advantageous to describe them in advance rather than in each individual story.

Anto	*Antonio Falsoni*	Well built with black hair, swarthy complexion. He had a husky voice and quite a strong personality. He lived and worked in his uncle's café, Uncle Luigi's. Good sense of humour and was the 'Bookie' of the gang.
Blackie	*Keith Havern*	Tall, well built, and athletic. Black short hair and always well dressed. A very good looking young man.
Boots	*Peter Markey*	Small, thin, with dark hair that always seemed to stick up at the crown of his head. A good footballer and loved wearing boots, hence the nickname.
Dunno	*Peter McManus*	Small, brown haired lad, best mate of Jumpy Jones. His answer to most questions was, 'Dunno'.

Ginger	*Thomas McVerry*	Small ginger haired lad with a round 'cheeky' face. A good footballer and runner. He was an excellent climber.
Jammy	*Tommy McAteer*	A dark haired, good looking lad who was an excellent footballer and a good all round athlete. He was fond of chatting up the girls. Very lucky or 'Jammy'.
Jumpy	*Francis Jones*	A tall skinny blond lad. Rivalled his mate Dunno in the brains department, but with a good sense of fun. Could never stand still and was always being asked to stop jumping around.
Lanky	*John Larkin*	A tall thin lad with large blue eyes and blond hair. Ungainly in posture but a good runner.
Naffy	*Leo McKay*	A small, mostly untidy, dark haired young man forever looking to borrow things, mostly money. A wheeler dealer.
Pajoe	*Patrick Joseph McArdle*	Red Morgan's uncle, small, grey haired stout man with a round ruddy face. Always in a jolly mood. Carpenter by trade.

Po	*Oliver Hillen*	Small with black curly hair, hooked nose and a swarthy complexion. He was the 'ideas' man of the gang, a few months older than Red. It was never discovered where the nickname 'Po' came from but Red suspected it had something to do with his 'Potty' when he was a baby.
Red	*John Joseph Morgan*	A tall, well built, athletic lad with a mass of red hair that was unkempt during the week, but well Brylcreemed for the dances at the weekends.
Roberto	*Roberto Falsoni*	Small, balding, swarthy, stubby man who worked in the café for Uncle Luigi, mostly with Ice Cream sales. In his early 40s. Uncle Luigi's son.
Shifty	*Jimmy McShane*	Small, brown haired, freckle faced young man who enjoyed gambling. Always on the look out for ways to make money.
The Bishop	*Peter Keenan*	Tall, rather studious lad with glasses. Dark blond hair, always neat, took pride in his dress. Everyone thought he looked like a clergyman. Good Chess player.
Topcoat	*James Anderson*	The odd one out in the gang. A small, thin, wizen faced man with a lisp and a mop of ginger hair. He was about 40 years old and lived in a little cottage on his own outside Camlough village. He would have been considered eccentric.

Places

Due to the fact that many of the same places appear in almost all the stories within, I hope it may be advantageous to describe them in advance rather than in each individual story.

Uncle Luigi's Cafe	Situated on Newry's main street, Luigi's was a local meeting place for all the gang. One of Red and Po's best friends, Anto Falsoni, worked there part-time for his uncle and café owner, Luigi Falsoni. The café had an ice cream counter on the left when entering. Next on the left was the Jukebox. On the right there were five 'Snugs' with high backed seats with a fixed table in the centre. On the left of the café was a collection of gingham covered tables and chairs. At the far end was the 'Chip Counter'. There could be found Luigi's pride and joy, the great glistening chrome chipper. It had a painted Italian beach scene on its upper part, and the same chipper was said to produce the best 'Fish and Chips' in Ireland.

The Bucket	An old, flat roofed hall found halfway along Castle Street at the corner of the hill of Hyde Market, directly facing the famous McCann's Bakery. The hall itself was said to have been originally the Abbot's house. There was a tunnel running from the building under Castle Street to the old Abbey grounds which was said to be the way the Abbot went every morning to say mass, as he was not allowed to be seen by the public. The dance floor was upstairs and was reached by a steep climb of thirty steps at the Hyde Market end. A large cross was positioned in front of the hall looking down towards the town.
The Florentine	Known as 'The Flo', it was located at the centre of Hill Street, a well known local, Italian owned café, famous for its frothy coffee and good quality food.
The Savoy Cinema	Located at the corner of Monaghan Street at the canal bridge. The most modern of the local cinemas, it was well known for its balcony, or as it was known locally, 'The Gods'.
The Imperial Cinema	Located on The Mall. The smallest of the local cinemas and without doubt, the most ancient. When the time came to start the movie, the ticket collector would walk to the stage and open the heavy velvet curtains to expose the screen to allow the movie to begin. Known locally as 'The Flea Pit'.

The Frontier Cinema	Located on John Mitchell Place, a continuation of Newry's Main Street, Hill Street. This was a favourite for a number of reasons. Firstly, it was only a few hundred yards from Castle Street. Secondly, Red and Po had found a way to gain entrance without having to pay. Thirdly, they had a morning session every Saturday in which there was a Talent Competition on stage for the local kids before the movie began. They also were well up to date on all the Serials, like The Lone Ranger, Superman, Batman and Robin, and such like.
The Nun's Graveyard	A large park type hillside behind St. Clare's Convent. It was surrounded by an eight foot wall. Inside the wall were well kept grassy areas with plants and many large oak trees and weeping willows. Looked upon as a 'spooky' place at night.
The Parochial Hall	Located at Downshire Road, near the Town Hall, this was a place which booked the top Showbands in Ireland. Every weekend it would be packed to hear music from The Royal, The Freshmen, The Miami, The College Boys, The Clipper Charlton and many more. No alcohol was served, just coffee, tea, soft drinks and milkshakes.

Newry Town Centre
1960

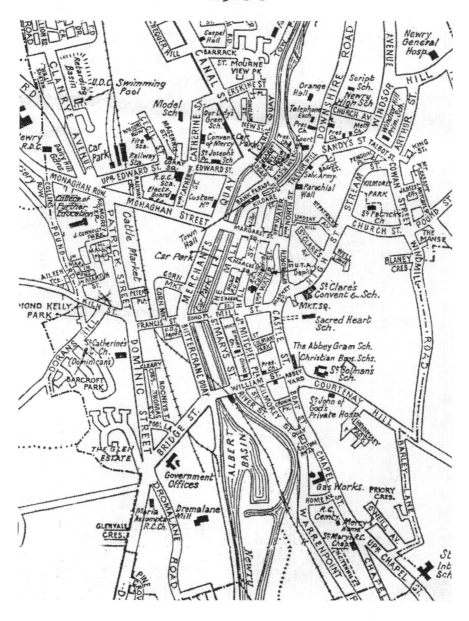

CONTENTS

The Electric Guitar

1960

"Happy Birthday," smiled Red, as he met Po walking along North Street.

Po looked down at his feet.

"Ahhh, sure he's all embarrassed."

"Piss off, you."

"Now Po, ya'll have ta start behavin' better than that, now that you're a big sixteen."

"Piss off, you."

"And, ya'll have ta stop that bad language, too, ya know."

"Frig off."

"My God, and here I am trying ta help ya with the growin' up stuff and this is what I get, sure, I'm cut ta the bone."

"Will ya shut your mouth, will ya? Oh listen, I got loads a presents, ya know."

"Ya did? Tell me?"

"I got a jumper from granny. I got a pair a trousers from the other granny. But the best present I got was from mom and dad."

"Well, what was it?"

"A guitar."

"Wow, ya got a real guitar?"

"Not just a guitar, but an electric one. It's called a Broadway."

"Well, lucky you. Have ya tried it out, yet?"

"No, not really, a just strummed it a little. It needs ta be plugged in and everythin' to hear it right, ya know."

"Sure, I knew that. So when are ya goin' ta have it all set up? I want ta hear it."

"Later."

They arrived at Uncle Luigi's Café and sat down in the first snug. Anto leaned over the counter with a broad grin across his face.

"How's the birthday boy?"

"Don't you start, shithead," snapped Po.

"Jasus, isn't that lovely. Ya wish one of your bestest friends in the whole world a happy birthday and he calls ya names," complained Anto, looking at Red.

"Sure, didn't I get the same my own self when I met him," said Red, holding out his arms pleadingly.

"I know yous bastards, ya know, yous will find some way ta take the piss. I know yis only too well."

"Ah now, de ya hear that, Red? An all the trouble we went ta for him."

"What trouble?"

"Don't even know if we should tell him, Red, what de ya think?"

"Ah sure, ya better, he'll only whinge in ma ear all day."

Anto disappeared for a moment and returned with a large parcel neatly wrapped in brown paper. He reached across the counter and handed it to Po.

"This is from Red and meself," smiled Anto.

"What's this?" a surprised Po managed to get out.

"Well, if ya open it ya'll see, ya ejit," said Red, smiling.

Po had the paper off in seconds. Inside, he found a dark blue hooded all-weather jacket. Not just any dark blue hooded all-weather jacket, but the very same jacket he stopped to look at every time he passed Kelly's Man's Shop window. He had pointed it out to Red about a dozen times.

"Oh, my God! Its ma jacket, the one I was after. This is it, the very one I wanted."

Po was on his feet in seconds and had all the labels off and had the jacket on. He was walking around, admiring himself with a great smile across his face.

"How did yous know this was the one I wanted?"

Red looked at Anto and took a deep breath.

"Just a wild guess," he smiled.

"This is fab! Great! The best present, yet. Thanks very much, lads."

"Anto, see if he kisses me, I'll punch him, I swear," said Red seriously.

Red was too late, Po had his arms around Red's neck and planted a big kiss on his cheek.

"Frig off will ya fruit. I told ya before not ta do that, people will think I'm a fruit like you," said Red, rubbing his cheek.

Po looked up at Anto who was standing behind the counter with a large carving knife in his hand.

"Don't even think about it," he growled at Po.

"Well, ya can take it off now, Po," said Red.

"No way, it's staying where it is. I have been admiring this jacket for yonks. I'm keeping it on."

"Children, they're all the same," said a straight-faced Red to Anto.

Later that day Red knocked Po's front door which, was promptly opened by his younger brother, Paul.

"He's in the kitchen," he shouted, and disappeared past Red into the street.

Red entered the hallway and went through to the kitchen, where he found Po and his mom sitting at the table. Red noticed one of Po's hands heavily bandaged.

"Jasus, Po, what happened ta your hand?"

"Well, ya may ask," snapped Po's mom. "He couldn't wait for his father to get home to set up the guitar for him. He had ta do it himself, didn't he?" she said, getting up from the table and leaving the room, mumbling to herself.

"So, what happened?" asked Red, sitting down.

"Stupid thing."

"What stupid thing?"

"The stupid guitar."

"Right, so what did this stupid guitar do, then?"

"Long story."

"So? Did ya ever tell a short one?"

"You're such a smart arse."

"Will ya tell me, will ya?"

"Well, me dad said he had another part for the guitar he had to pick up, ya see."

"Yeah?"

"Well, sure I only wanted ta hear it like, ya know?"

"Yeah?"

"Well, I put a plug on the thing, plugged it in."

"Jasus, I think I see where this is goin'."

"Well, sure it blew me across the kitchen, so it did."

"Ya plugged the guitar directly into the mains?"

"Yeah."

"Ya moron! Ya plug the guitar into an amplifier, so ya do. Even I know that."

"Well, I know that too . . . now."

Red put his face into his hands.

✳   ✳   ✳

Later that day, and perhaps somewhat unfortunately, for Po, Red had arrived at Uncle Luigi's before he did. That evening the story of Po's little accident with the guitar had somehow managed to get around. Po had to walk the gauntlet from the door to the top counter.

"I hear you lit up the street with your new guitar, Po," smiled Jumpy.

"Will ya play us something with a bit of a kick to it, Po?" added the Bishop.

"I heard he was only a flash in the pan," put in Dunno.

"Is it true ya can make sparks come outta your guitar, Po?" asked Jammy.

"I heard that when ya play Po, the whole place lights up," smirked Kitter.

Po never turned his head, he just kept walking until he reached the counter and the safety of the first snug, where he found the grinning faces of Red, Anto and Topcoat.

"Total friggin' bastard whore," snarled Po at Red.

"Jasus, what did I do?"

"Ya had to tell all them bastards, didn't ya?"

"Ach, Po, it just sorta slipped out, so it did."

"I'll slip somethin' in, my fist into your big mouth."

"Well, Po," intervened Anto, standing up and raising his hands in the air.

"We wish you a shocking Birthday," sang the well-rehearsed patrons of Uncle Luigi's.

"Bastards, friggin' whores, the lot of ya," muttered Po, playing with his bandaged hand.

"With friends like yous, who needs enemies?"

End

One Tooth Pete

1960

Red and Po were walking along Hill Street in Newry on that Thursday evening chatting about Co. Down's big match in the Ulster Final this coming Sunday. The match would be played in Clones, against Co. Cavan, with the winners to go into the All Ireland Semi Final against Offaly at Dublin's Croke Park.

"We have by far the better forwards so we have," stated Po.

"I'm not arguing with that, what I am sayin' is, that Cavan have one of the strongest defences in the country," said Red.

"I know that, but do ya think they will hold Paddy Docherty, or Breen Morgan or Sean O'Neill? No chance."

The conversation was interrupted by the evening paper man, selling his papers outside the Imperial Hotel.

"Belfast Tele, Belfast Tele, Down in Sundays Ulster Final," came the high pitched voice of 'One Tooth Pete'. He had acquired the name ten years ago when two of his last three teeth were removed. He only had one tooth left now, on the top, right at the front of his mouth and refused to have it removed, however black it had become. Pete was perhaps a little mentally deprived it could be said.

"Hi Pete," smiled Po.

"Hello Po and hello Red. How are ya all doing? Are ya goin' on Sunday are ya?"

"Of course," replied Red. "Wouldn't miss it for the world."

"Yis are lucky buggers, wish I could go."

"You're not goin' Pete?" inquired Po, sitting down on the footpath and looking through the evening paper.

"Jasus, can't make up the friggin' fare so a can't. Would need to sell a hell of a lot more papers ta make the money."

"Ah well, sure ya never know. Somethin' exciting might happen and ya might sell loads of papers before the weekend," smiled Red starting to walk away.

Po decided he would buy the paper for the football section. Pete refused the money and told him to have it.

When Po caught up with Red he remarked, "Poor One Tooth, he is a nice guy."

"That he is, if a had the money a would give it ta him ma own self."

Suddenly Po stopped. He was reading something inside the paper.

"Jasus, sure don't I only have an idea."

"Oh no, here comes trouble."

"Come on back to One Tooth."

"What are ya up ta now ya wee bugger?"

Po just smiled. When they reached One Tooth, Po approached him and asked . . .

"How many more papers would ya need ta sell ta go ta the match?"

"Shit, at least fifty or more, why?"

"I have an idea, but ya will have ta do exactly as I say, right?"

"Ok . . . what is it?"

Po folded up the paper and pointed to a report near the bottom of page four.

"De ya see that?" he asked One Tooth.

"Ahhh, naked woman arrested running on Birmingham's Hill Street."

"Good, now leave out the Birmingham."

"What?"

"Are ya deaf, leave out the Birmingham will ya?"

"What the hell are ya on about Po?" asked Red moving closer.

"Will yis listen will yis? Instead of you shouting 'Belfast Tele,' shout, 'Naked woman arrested on Hill Street', get it?"

Red roared laughing.

"I friggin' get it, I get it. A love it."

As Red and Po walked away they could hear the loud voice of One Tooth.

"Naked woman arrested on Hill Street."

They could also hear the voices of passers by.

"A paper please."

"One for me too."

That Sunday on the train to the match in Clones, Red and Po got a cigarette each as a thank you from One Tooth who sold his extra papers and managed the fare.

"Another good deed to add to my growing list," smiled Po.

"A have ta admit, it was a good one for sure. What put it into your head anyway?" smiled Red.

"Sure I was just thinkin', ya see, people love ta see other people in trouble, and if they know them, it's ten times better. All them ones that bought the extra papers were hopin' it was someone they knew ya see."

"I see, so like, when we are doing a composition in school, and I write about someone I know gettin' his wee willie caught in his zipper, a might get extra marks?"

"Don't even think about it bastard face."

Down won the match and were now Ulster Champions.

End

A Dog's Life

1960

Red was lying on his bed reading his favourite comic, The Topper. He looked up as the door to his bedroom opened. His best friend Po was standing there with a sombre look on his face.

"What's wrong?"

Po looked down at his feet.

"Rascal's dead," he mumbled.

"Jasus! What happened Po?"

"I found him on the street near our house. I think he was hit by a car."

Red was looking at Po's face. He could see his eyes filling up. He got up and walked over to him, putting his arm around Po's shoulder he tried to find some words to comfort his friend.

"Ya know, he most likely didn't feel a thing. He probably died instantly ya know, so at least he had no pain."

"I was hopin' that's what happened my own self. Did ya know he was almost ten years old our Rascal?"

"Was he really, I didn't think he was that old."

"We had some great times together so we did. Do ya remember that time he got his head stuck in the railings? The auld ejit was after a cat."

"I remember that so a do," laughed Red.

"An what about that time he jumped at auld Mrs. Hogan and she dropped her groceries all over the street."

Po was smiling now, remembering the good times he had with his friend, Rascal.

"Red, will ya give me a hand to bury him?"

"Jasus Po, sure ya know a will, that goes without sayin'. Anto and the lads will come along too so they will, they all liked Rascal."

"Do ya think I should get a box made for him, a mean, it wouldn't be like, too much, would it?"

"I think that's a great idea. Leave it with me and I will get our Pajoe ta start on it right away. When are ya plannin' ta bury him and where?"

"I was thinkin', up the 'Rocks' on High Street. He loved going up there."

"Ok, I will call for ya at three o'clock. I'll have the box an all by then. I'll get all the lads to meet us on the 'Rocks'. Anto will get his Uncle Roberto to drive us up there."

"That would be great, thanks Red."

"Not a problem."

Red did indeed get the little box made for Rascal and Pajoe even printed his name on the top. All the gang had been informed and promised to turn up for Rascal's funeral. Red, Anto and Po placed the body of Rascal in the box and laid it gently, with great decorum, into the boot of Roberto's car, who then drove to the High Street Rocks. They took the box out of the car and started the climb up the steep grassy gradient until they reached the top. There they found the whole gang waiting quietly. The entire ceremony was very dignified. Red said a few words as did Anto and Jumpy. Po was the last to speak and had a hard job holding back the tears. He recalled Rascal's life from when he was a tiny pup and some of the funny things he did and how he loved playing with the children on the street. He knew all their names too Po pointed out.

So Rascal was laid to rest. His grave was on the highest point of the 'Rocks', overlooking the town. The mourners then began the long trek back down the hill.

"The wee brother will crack up when he hears about Rascal ya know. He's away fishing at the County River and he doesn't know yet," Po said to Red.

"Wow, he will take it hard for sure," said Red.

They had just reached the bottom of the grassy slope when Jumpy spoke
to Po.
"Did a hear ya say that your wee brother was away fishing?"
"Yeah, why?"
"Isn't that him over there playing football?"
Po and Red both looked in the direction of a group of lads playing football
and Jumpy was indeed correct, Po's little brother was there.
"I suppose a better go and tell him, will ya come with me Red?"
"Sure, come on."

Po called his young brother who arrived breathlessly.
"I'm afraid I have ta talk ta ya about Rascal," said Po in a soft voice.
"Jasus, did mom find out, did she? Shit, I'm in trouble now so a am."
"What are ya talkin' about?"
"Rascal, isn't that what you are talkin' about? I took him with me earlier
when a went fishin'. Mom won't let me take him cause she's afraid he will
run out on the road and get knocked down."
"Hold on a minute, ya took Rascal fishin' with ya?"
"Isn't that what I'm sayin'. There he is over there playin' with Rooney's
dog."
Red and Po looked in the direction of the barking and there was Rascal
indeed having a great time with Rooney's dog.
"Can't be, he's dead," Po managed to get out.
"Who's dead?" Po's brother asked.
"Rascal's dead, he was knocked down on North Street this morning, we
just buried him."
"I see what happened, ya thought that dog on North Street was Rascal?
Jasus, you're nuts our fella. That was Docherty's dog, Jip. He was killed
early this morning. Come ta think of it, he does look very like our Rascal,
doesn't he? I'm away back ta play football, see ya later."
Red looked at Po and started to giggle. The giggle grew, and grew, into
uncontrollable fits of laughter. He had to sit down.
"Frig me . . . I don't believe it . . . I just don't believe . . . we buried
Docherty's dog . . . ," Red managed to get out.
"It's not that funny Morgan ya bastard," Po snapped.
"You . . . will . . . never . . . ever . . . live this down, ya know that, don't
ya?" Red got out.

Later Red, Anto and Po were sitting in Uncle Luigi's drinking coffee.

"Ya know Po, you are a right ejit, do ya know that?" said Anto laughing.
"All right, all right, for Christ sake, don't you start. I got enough from dickhead here," snapped Po nodding towards a broadly smiling Red.
"But Po, think about it, ya buried Docherty's dog thinking it was yours, a mean, ya'r definitely off your trolley," pointed out Anto.
"Look, anyone could have made that mistake so they could. The two dogs could have been twins," complained Po.
"Ah well, sure it's all over now, at least Docherty's dog got a fine send off with Po crying over his coffin," smirked Red.
"This is true, very true," laughed Anto.
"Well, wee Po, I have ta be goin'. Now don't be lookin' so sad, everything turned out ok in the end, didn't it?" said Red sliding out of the snug.
"Yeah, I suppose so, but you bastards will never let it go will ya?"
Red leaned over and patted Po on the shoulder.
"There, there Po, I know how your wee self feels, sure it's a dog's life."
Anto roared laughing and had to get out of the snug.
"Yous are a bunch of whores and bastards the whole lot of ya."

End

Jumpy's Big Day

1960

About once a month someone would organize an inter-street football match. These matches were usually against Boat Street, High Street or O'Neill Avenue. They would be played in a field beside Newry Town Football Club's ground. This month a match was arranged with Boat Street. Kick-off was scheduled for Sunday afternoon at 3pm.

There were no colours, and no football kits. Most of the boys would be lucky to own a pair of football boots. Team numbers, too, were quite flexible. It was really down to whoever turned up. For example, if one side had twelve men and the other had ten, the team with the greater number would give one of their players to the other side.

"How many's turnin' up, then?" Red asked Po, as they walked along the Warrenpoint Road.
"I make it nine and a half," said Po.
"Nine and a half?"
"Yeah, Jumpy's playin'."
"He's less than useless, even on a dry day."
"He's not worth a rat's fart," smiled Po.

They both stopped walking and stood facing each other.

"He's as useful as an ashtray on a motorbike."

"He's as good as a one legged tap dancer."

"He wouldn't make sub on a disabled girl's team."

"He would be the worst player on a one man team."

"I have seen people play better with no legs."

"He has two left feet."

"Or two right feet."

"Or two wrong feet."

"He could play better with no feet."

"He is as useful as a rubber nail."

"He is as useful as a plastic toastin' fork."

"He is as useless as . . . ."

"Wow . . . stop. If he is all that bad, why do we let him play, then?" asked Red.

"He turns up . . . and . . . he always has toffee!"

"Ok, yeah, forgot about that."

Ten minutes later the two reached the football field, still discussing Jumpy. The goals were set up on both sides. On the Castle Street side, a coat and a duffle bag was used, on the Boat Street side, a coat and a jumper. A member from the opposing team paced out the distance of the opposition goals to ensure fairness. When he left, and his back was turned, the goals were obviously made smaller. The coin was tossed and the game got under way. There was great rivalry between Boat Street and Castle Street in all sports events, football, of course, being the most important.

The game today was, as expected, very close with much arguing, shouting, pushing, swearing, threats and occasional fighting. Because there were no goal posts, as such, most of the arguing was about whether the ball passed on the inside or the outside of the 'coat'. The official 'Match Timer' was, in fact, a very exalted position, held by only four people that year. These were the only four people available who actually owned a watch. Today it was Bap Foy, from Boat Street, who was the official timekeeper. On these occasions time was known to be stretched, or in some cases, shortened, depending on whether the timekeeper's favourite team was winning or losing.

There was a corner kick to Castle Street in the dying minutes of the game. Before the kick was taken both teams checked with the timekeeper and it was agreed there was just one minute left in the game, and the score was 6—6.

Po placed the ball carefully and stepped back to take the kick. There was much pushing and shoving in the goalmouth with Castle Street needing to score to win and Boat Street needing to keep the ball out of the goal to achieve a draw.

Most of the Castle Street team were hovering in and around the Boat Street goalmouth. Jumpy, too, was right in the middle as ordered by the captain, Po.

"Jumpy, stay in the middle. Ya can at least put someone off," barked Po.

Jumpy did as he was told and looked like a real forward moving and dodging about in the goalmouth area. Po took the kick. The ball, looped across toward the middle of the Boat Street goal. Kitter Murray, Castle Street's best forward felt he could get his head to the ball but found that Jumpy was in the way.

"Jumpy . . . leave it . . . move . . . !" shouted Kitter.

Jumpy turned towards Kitter.

"What?"

As he did so, the ball hit him on the forehead, took off at an angle, and into the Boat Street goal. The word 'goal' seemed to be screamed from all the Castle Street team at the same time. There was great celebrating and cheering as Jumpy's team-mates mobbed him. Jumpy describes the goal to this day as a perfectly executed move. The ball was met with precision and determination, angled into the corner of the goal with uncanny accuracy and power. The rest of the team would just swap glances and smile when Jumpy related this story to anyone who would listen. There's a lot to be said for being in the right place at the right time.

End

The Storyteller

1960

Red was on his way out of the front door when he heard his mom's voice calling him.

"Come back here a minute, mister."

"What'd I do, now?"

"Nothin' . . . and you'd better not. Are you goin' to the storytellin' tonight?"

"Yeah."

"Who's goin' with ya?"

"Po."

"Have yous Cap Money?"

(Cap Money – Money collected in a flat cap for the Storyteller at the end of the evening.)

"No."

"Did your dad not give ya money?"

"Was that Cap Money? I spent it, I just thought he was givin' it ta me ta spend."

"Here's a shillin', now ya better let me see ya puttin' that in the cap tonight . . . do ya hear me?"

"I will . . . I will . . . honest."

"Ya better . . . I'm warnin' ya," she said pointing a threatening finger at Red's face.

Ten minutes later Red met up with the rest of the gang, outside Uncle Luigi's.

"Po, my mom reminded me on the way out about Cap Money. Have ya got yours?"

"Yeah, of course I have. De ya think I'm a spendthrift like you, de ya?"

"Piss off."

"Who all's goin'?"

"Just me, you and Anto, as far as I know."

"Lookin' forward to seein' auld Charlie, again. He must be some age now?"

"Jasus, he must be in his sixties, for sure."

"Remember last summer, the stories were great, weren't they?"

"Great night, I remember it well."

"I don't know how you guys can sit and listen to some auld fella tellin' stories all night," put in Jumpy Jones.

Red and Po exchanged glances.

"These rabble have no taste, do they, Red?" remarked Po, in his best snooty voice.

"Do ya know, you're right, Po. Even callin' them rabble is bein' nice ta them."

This got Red a thump on the arm from Jumpy, who took off at speed fearing retaliation.

Later that night Red and Po arrived at the Scout Hall to find a good crowd had already gathered. Every year old Charlie O'Donaghue would arrive in Newry and stay for around a week, having sittings every night at a different location, usually Pubs, but one night he would use the old Scout Hall, to enable the young people and the women to come and hear the stories. Red spotted Charlie talking to some men at the far end of the hall. He looked the same as he remembered him. His face, lined deeply by both weather and age had a grey pallor. His dark eyes, sunk beneath great bushy eyebrows darted about the room while he was in conversation. Occasionally, he waved to a familiar face, allowing tobacco-stained teeth to appear between thin lips. He was wearing the same old tweed coat and brown trousers he had worn last year. His collarless grey striped shirt was buttoned up, making his neck seem almost too small to hold his great head, which was covered in a mass of black, unkempt, greasy hair.

"Sit here, Red."
Red turned and looked at Po, startled.
"Here, here . . . sit here."
"Oh . . . right."
"Where were you just then?"
"Miles away."
"Here's Anto comin' now," said Po, looking over his shoulder.
"Well," panted Anto, as he arrived beside Red.
"Where were you, then? Thought we were ta meet at Castle Street?"
"Crowd came in and I had ta help out. Jasus, is that Billy McGrath over there?"
"Yeah, why?" answered Red.
"He looks like death warmed up, so he does."
"De ya know what, Red, he's worse than an auld one, so he is, passin' remarks about people."
"I know, wouldn't ya think he'd mind his own business?"
"Wouldn't ya just?"

"Right now ladies and gentlemen, boys and girls, can I have your attention, please," came the booming voice of Johnny Crimmins, the local scout master, from the small stage at the top of the hall.
"Thank you . . . thank you. I have the honour tonight once again, to introduce one of Ireland's best known and loved storytellers. Every year he comes to see us and every year he brings us new and exciting stories about our beloved land and its people. This year, I am sure, he will once again entertain us as only he can. Ladies and gentlemen, boys and girls, will you give a warm Newry welcome to Ireland's own . . . Charlie O'Donaghue."
There was loud and prolonged applause and cheering as Charlie walked, slowly, smiling and waving, to the centre of the stage, where an armchair and table had been placed. There was a microphone placed on a stand in front of the chair. Sitting down, with some effort, Charlie coughed into a blue-edged handkerchief and took a drink from the glass of stout he had brought with him.
"Good evenin' ta ya all," came the clear southern accented voice.
"Good evenin', Charlie," came the combined reply.

"Well now, sure don't ya know a love comin' back ta auld Newry. When a came under the bridge at Cloghogue, a stopped and looked down into the Valley of the Yews at this beautiful and historical town and it's with that picture in mind that I will begin my story for you all tonight. Now, the story begins a little away from here in the town of Kinsale, not a stone's throw from the great city of Cork, where there was a great battle in the year of our Lord, 1601. It was said that over twelve hundred souls were killed, both, during that battle and even fleein' from it, by the army of a nice English gentleman, named Sir Arthur Chichester. All, as the story goes, were decapitated by the English army on the orders of Sir Arthur. Our English friend advocated a ruthless policy across the whole of Ireland. A policy of destruction and terror that, before long also became the policy of another nice English gentleman, Lord Mountjoy. But it has ta be said that some of the worst scenes of horror were in the Newry area."

Charlie stopped and took a sip of his stout. He took a deep breath and continued.

"One night, near their camp, said to be situated in the Church Street area, Chichester's soldiers encountered a peculiar odour comin' from a wood near their camp. It was like the roastin' or broilin' of meat, it was said."

Charlie smiled, looking around his audience.

"Now, would there be anyone here from Church Street area tonight?"

A number of hands went up, mostly women.

"Ah, I see. So it's true then, Church Street women are the most beautiful in Newry."

This got a few cheers and a round of applause.

Charlie continued.

"Later that night a young girl, by all reports, in terror, ran into the camp and reported she had escaped from three old witches in the woods. She said that some of her friends and herself were enticed to the camp of the old women, who surprised them, killed her friends, cut them up and began cookin' them. She barely escaped with her life. A number of soldiers were dispatched to the area of the woods the girl described, where they found a cabin. There, they came across the three old ladies cookin' human flesh. The women were duly executed for their crime.

On many occasions, in later years, reports of the cries of children in the night were made by people livin' in the area. Some even claim to have seen wailin' children walkin' in the dark of night, some missin' a limb, and some it was said, were headless."

19

There were some gasps from the audience. Red looked across at Po who was sitting pale-faced with mouth open, staring at the storyteller. He laughed to himself thinking of how he would tease him afterwards.

Two more stories were duly told, not as gruesome as the first it must be said, which left the listeners in a more joyous mood at the end.

On leaving the hall Red was in the company of both Po and Anto as they walked along the now dark Boat Street.

"Wasn't that somethin' about the eatin' of them children . . . Jasus," said Anto, in a sort of hushed voice.

"That's the last time I'll be in Church Street after dark, I can tell ya," added Red.

"De ya think it was true about the old witches, then?" asked Anto.

"Definitely, for sure," said Red, with some conviction.

"You're very quiet, Po. Did auld Charlie scare your wee self, did he?" asked Anto.

"Friggin' sure, he did. Don't tell me he didn't scare you."

"Well, I suppose he did, but not as badly as you. A mean, sure look at the state of ya. You're shakin' in your boots," laughed Anto.

"Will ya leave our Po alone, Anto. The wee man will have enough ta contend with when he passes Lindsey Hill. That's where a heard they saw a headless, wee boy."

"Frig off, Red, that's not funny, so it's not," said Po, seriously.

"Not funny, but true," added Anto.

"Well, sure ya can tell us all about it in the mornin', Po. Now, if ya see a ghost will ya ask it if the soldiers left any gold behind, an' if they did, where it is?" said Red.

"And, don't forget, Po. Don't turn your back on the ghost. That's the one thing I was told ya mustn't do," added Anto.

"Yous two are the funniest guys I've ever met, de ya know that?" snarled Po.

His reply was just laughter from both his companions.

Anto said goodnight at the top of William Street, where he branched off for home. Red and Po continued on into Castle Street.

"Will ya not come down ta my house for a wee while?" asked Po, looking at the ground.

"Naw, not tonight, have ta give me da a hand with somethin' when a go home. Why, are ya afraid ta go down North Street by your wee self then, Po, in case ya see a Bogey Man?"

"Piss off."

"Never worry. Sure, if a ghost gets ya, I'll go ta your wake, so a will, and say nice things about ya."

Just then a door banged on Castle Street, a few yards away, and a startled cat screeched loudly. The sounds were exaggerated in the stillness of the night. Red was the first to react. He jumped and grabbed Po by the shoulder. They both stopped. Po began laughing as he stepped back and pointed at Red.

"Ya big baby," he laughed. "Wait till a tell Anto, tomorrow, about the big brave Red who jumped three feet in the air when a big bad pussy cat scared him."

"You'll say nothin' of the sort, ya wee frigger," snapped Red.

"Are ya goin' ta stop me, ya big baby, then," laughed Po, as he danced in front of Red.

Red tried to catch him, but it was a lost cause. He almost caught him halfway along North Street, just about hundred yards from Po's house.

Po looked behind and stopped when he saw Red stopped with hands on knees sucking in air.

"Jasus, thanks Morgan. That was really nice of ya."

"What was?" panted Red.

"For leavin' me home. Really nice of ya."

Red looked around and realised he had in fact done just that.

"I'll get ya tomorra ya wee bugger."

"Now watch yourself on the way home now Red. Be careful passin' them auld dark entryways, a have heard bad stories about a wee headless boy so a have."

"Bastard."

"Night shitface," smiled Po.

End

The Talking Fish

1960

"Get a grip Anto, they wouldn't go for it," said Red seriously.
"Wanna bet? Remember, it's Dunno and Jumpy we're talkin' about ya know," said Anto.
"Good point. But de ya really think they'll believe it?"
"It's a dead cert."
"This I have ta see," laughed Red.
"I'll set the stage with a few stories or somethin' ta get them goin'."
"Ok, what time de ya want me ta be here?"
"Just the usual, about closin'. Tell Po ta be here too."
"Ok, see ya later."

Later that day, Red related Anto's plan to Po.
"Yeah, they're stupid enough ta go for it, I can just see it now," laughed Po.
"So, Anto wants us to be there about closin' time."
"Wouldn't miss it for a barrel of ice cream," sniggered Po.
"I'm not so sure they'll go for it ya know. Ok, they're not the brightest lights on the Christmas tree, but a Fish Ghost? That's pushin' the boat out."

"I'm tellin' ya, them two ejits will believe every word Anto tells them," said Po.

*   *   *

The cleaning was all done that night and everyone was seated in the front snug finishing their chips at Uncle Luigi's.

"I looked that up for ya Red in Roberto's encyclopaedia," said Anto.

"Ya did? What did it say?"

"Well, I didn't read it all, there were pages and pages about it, but ya were right, hundreds of people have reported seein' Fish Ghosts."

"There ya go, I told ya," said Red triumphantly. "My grandda swears by it, he says there was a big pike out in the County River. For years every fisherman in the area tried to get it on a hook, then about ten years ago a guy from Mayobridge caught it. He got it stuffed and it's now hangin' in some bar or other."

"And did it come back?" asked Anto.

"It sure did. It was seen dozens of times after that."

"Sure it could have been another fish," said Dunno.

"No, it was the same pike. Ya see it had very unusual markin's."

"I don't believe that for a minute, a Fish Ghost!" sneered Jumpy.

"Well, it's the truth, even Roberto has seen one ya know," said Anto.

"When was this?" asked Red.

"Oh, it was about a year ago. He was out in the kitchen one night gettin' the fish ready and one of them said hello to him."

"A dead fish?" gasped Dunno.

"Bin dead and on ice for days."

"Shit."

"The fish said hello ta him?" Jumpy asked disbelievingly.

"Just as bold as brass, looked up at him and said 'Hello there'."

"Frig me, that's somethin' all right," said a shocked Dunno.

"Anyway, talkin' of fish, will you guys give us a hand with the fish in the kitchen?"

"No bother," answered Dunno and Jumpy.

Red caught Anto's wink and had to pretend a coughing fit to stifle the laugh.

"Here's the keys to the van lads, will ya bring in the two empty boxes in the back?"

Jumpy and Dunno went out to the back where the van was parked.

"Jasus, they're goin' for it, the two ejits," laughed Po.

"Now Po, quick as ya can, get in there under the table."

All three hurried into the kitchen. Po got under the large table and Red and Anto placed some empty boxes in front of him which concealed his presence.

Anto opened a box and took out a large cod, placing it on the table.

"Where's the hole?" asked Red.

"There," said Anto pointing at a hole in the centre of the table.

"There was a big knot in the wood, fell out this mornin'."

"Here Po," said Anto, handing him a long wooden spoon through a space at the side of the boxes.

"Can ya see the hole?"

"Wait a minute . . . yeah . . . I have it . . . put the fish on it now."

Anto placed the fish on the table covering the hole. Po pushed the handle of the spoon through the hole. The fish's head lifted up.

"Friggin' brilliant," laughed Anto.

"It'll work a treat," added Red.

"Here they're comin' . . . shush."

"Where will we put these Anto?"

"Just throw them over there."

"Where's Po?" Dunno asked.

"Away home. Listen, Red and me have ta bring over some ice from the big freezer. Will ya pack up them boxes there against the wall?"

"Ok, no bother."

Red and Anto left through the kitchen door, but leaving it open enough to be able to hear what was going on inside. Nothing happened the next few minutes. The two boys just chatted generally.

"Po does great voices, doesn't he?" whispered Anto.

"He should be on the stage," giggled Red.

"What was that?" asked Jumpy stopping what he was doing.

"What was what?"

"Shush . . . listen."

There was a slapping sound coming from the table.

"It's comin' from over there," said Dunno.

Both were now staring at the table. Suddenly the large cod's head lifted up as if it was looking at them.

"Hello boys," came the deep booming voice.

Jumpy and Dunno almost took the kitchen door off its hinges in their haste to get out. Luckily, Red and Anto had moved quickly away from the door and pretended they were on their way back. The boys both shouted to Red and Anto. "Friggin' run for it."

Red and Anto followed the two boys out into the now darkened café. They were standing with hands on knees breathing heavily.

"What happened?" asked Red innocently.

"Ya won't friggin' believe it Red . . . ya just won't."

"What?" asked Anto.

"You tell them Dunno."

"No . . . you tell them."

"Will one of yis friggin' tell us?"

"We . . . ya won't believe it Anto. We were stackin' the boxes . . . right?"

"Right."

"We heard this noise . . . ya know . . . like a slap."

"A slap?"

"That's what it was like, so we were lookin' over at the table . . . and the friggin' fish moved."

"You're tryin' ta wind us up now Dunno," smirked Red.

"I swear to God . . . you tell them Jumpy."

"I saw it too, no jokin'. The fish lifted its head and looked at us so it did."

"Right, sure it did, and ya'll be tellin' us next it said hello," laughed Anto.

"It friggin' did . . . it said 'Hello boys'. Didn't it Dunno?"

"I swear ta God," said Dunno making a small cross with his finger on his neck. "It said hello."

"The big cod on the table?"

"Yeah."

"It said hello?"

"Yeah."

Anto looked at Red. "What do ya think of that Red?"

"Sounds a bit fishy ta me."

That was too much for Anto. He could not hold it in any longer. He just sat down and roared. Red did not need any encouragement to join him.

At that moment Po arrived.

"Hello boys," he boomed in a deep voice.

Dunno and Jumpy swapped glances as Po joined his two convulsing mates.

"Ya friggin' bastards."

"Whores."

Later when they were all seated and somewhat calmed down, Anto looked at Red.

"Ya were right, it was a bit fishy."

"We reeled them in well," added Po.

"Hook, line and sinker," laughed Red.

"Tell ya what . . . we made a right 'cod' of them," laughed Anto.

Jumpy stood up.

"Are ya comin' home Dunno? These friggers are doin' ma head in."

"Yeah, mine too. They think they're funny so they do."

The two walked toward the door.

"Ach boys, now will ya not have a cod and chip before ya go?"

The answers were predictable.

End

Visit to the Doctor

1960

"No way. I'm not sittin' in a stupid friggin' Doctor's waitin' room for an hour waitin' on you," complained Red.

"No, my doctor is really fast. Ya never have ta wait very long. Come on, Red, please? Pretty please?" pleaded Po.

"Look, I'll go with ya. If I have ta wait more than 15 minutes I'm gone, right?"

"Right."

"So, tell me again, why ya have ta see him," asked Red.

"He is goin' ta make my willie 3 inches longer."

"Really, so ya will have a 3 ½ inch willie then? Well, at least ya'll be able ta see it."

"Ah, very funny."

This reply got Red a hard punch on the arm, which made him groan.

"Frig off, ya wee bugger, that was sore."

"Well, it wasn't meant ta tickle."

"So, tell me why ya'r goin' ta see him?"

"It's that time I scratched ma knee playin' football. It just won't heal up. Keeps gettin' worse. It has got infected, too."

"He won't want ta be wastin' time with that. He'll just amputate the leg and be done with it."

"Ya'r such a comfort Morgan. Sure, I don't know who I would go ta for a bit of sympathy, if it wasn't for you. Maybe Joey Loughran's pet snake would be next in line."

That afternoon Red and Po entered the waiting room of Dr. John McCaffery. There were a few people already there. Red recognized a couple of them. The room was a dull, dingy place with a strong smell of polish and disinfectant. A fringed, faded, red-flowered carpet covered the centre of the small room with a well polished oval coffee table in the centre, laden with magazines. Heavy, green satin curtains did their best to keep the room in semi darkness.

"I hate these places," Red whispered to Po.

"Why? Sure, they have everythin' ya could want here. See those magazines on the table? They're for the patients over a hundred years old. They were published during the war. See these chairs and them there curtains, and that there carpet? Well they were made at the end of World War One. And all just ta make the old patients feel at home."

"So what is there for us, then?"

"Jasus, you're blind, so ya are. Didn't ya see the receptionist's legs?"

"Of course a did."

"And?"

"They're nice."

"Nice? They're fantastic."

The waiting room silence was broken by a sustained and loud outburst of coughing from an elderly man seated in the corner.

"How much longer do we friggin' have ta wait here? I'll end up with friggin' leprosy or somthin'," whispered Red, in a serious voice.

"Get a grip, will ya. Ya auld edjit."

"Mr. Hillen, please?" came the soft voice of 'legs'.

"Here," said Po, standing and following the receptionist from the waiting room. His eyes were firmly fixed on her lower extremities.

Po entered the Doctor's surgery and was motioned by Dr. McCaffery to a seat at the end of his desk. After a moment or two the Doctor looked up.

"Well, Mr. Hillen, and what seems to be the problem?"

"It's my knee again, Doctor. It's not healing a'tall."

"Ok. Drop your trousers and let's have a look, then."

Po stood and did as he was asked. The doctor knelt down and gently removed the bandage from around Po's knee.

"Let's see now, hmm . . . , it does seem to be infected all right. We'll have to do something about that right away. Stay where you are a moment."

The doctor went to a large cupboard on the other side of his surgery and returned shortly with what seemed to Po to be the biggest needle he had ever seen. He felt the blood drain from his face.

"Bend over now, like a good man."

Po slowly bent forward, taking hold of the edge of the desk.

"Ok now, just a little prick and it will be all over."

Po closed his eyes tightly, waiting for the pain. He felt the needle enter his buttock. It was quite painful and he flinched slightly.

"There now, not all that bad now, was it?"

He felt the doctor rubbing the area he had just injected.

'Not all that bad?' Po mocked the doctor's comment to himself. 'And how the shit would you know? You were on the other end.'

Po's buttock was indeed very painful but he refused to show it. The doctor replaced the bandage on Po's knee with a fresh one.

"Well now, let's see. I want you to come back again on . . . ah . . . Monday, at 3pm and we will see how we are getting on. Get this prescription filled today and take one tablet tonight and one every four hours starting tomorrow."

Po thanked the doctor and left the surgery. He motioned to Red in the Waiting Room and they both left together.

Outside, Po began his litany of complaints.

"Friggin' bastardin' whorein' shit," Po spat out while rubbing his backside.

"Jasus Po, was he a fruit?"

"Would ya ever piss off, ya whore. He stuck a friggin' knittin' needle in me arse. Says he, 'you'll only feel a wee prick'. Bollocks, it was like he stabbed me with a screwdriver."

"Ya poor wee person, sure, aren't ya very brave altogether. Hi, that's funny," laughed Red.

"What's friggin' funny?"

"A wee prick gets a wee prick."

"Jasus, you're such a comic, so ya are. If it had'a been you, ya would have fainted, so ya would."

"Not a'tall, No way. I'll bet it was only a wee jab ya got, ya baby. And sure, there I was in that friggin' waitin' room with no one ta talk to, only 'legs' herself."

"You're a lying bastard. Ya weren't talkin' ta her."

"I was so, an guess what? Didn't a only get a date for Friday night."

"Ya'r a lyin' slob, so ya are."

"Don't believe me, then."

"Ya'r serious?"

"Would I lie about somethin' as serious as this?"

"Jasus Christ, I don't believe it. I'm in there sufferin' pure agony and you, my so-called best mate, are chattin' up the receptionist."

"What can a tell ya. Did ya want me ta just sit there and see which one of them auld fogies had the best cough?"

"Well ya might have given a bit a thought ta me, sufferin' in there like a was."

"Sure, ya never left my mind. I was askin' Alice, that's her name by the way, if she would like to come ta the Pictures with me on Friday night. And all the time, sure, wasn't I worried out of my brain about what tortures ya were endurin' in there."

"Jasus, ya know what? Ya are a low down, sneaky, bastardin' . . . ."

"I suppose then ya don't want ta hear about Kathleen, then?"

"The wee dark haired one?"

"That's her."

"What about her?"

"Naw, ya wouldn't want ta hear, especially from me, your 'ex' friend, the whorein' bastardin' . . . . ."

"Will ya tell me, will ya?"

"Well sure, wasn't I only thinkin' of your poor wee self gettin' the big knittin' needle and got Alice to ask Kathleen if she would like ta make it a double date."

"And . . . what the hell did she say?"

"Who?"

"Kathleen, for frig sake."

"Oh, her. She said ok."

"Jasus."

"No, dopey, Kathleen."

"You're such a smart bastard, Morgan. Are ya tellin' the truth?"

"Yeah, we have a double date for Friday."

"Well frig me."

"Not a chance."

Po's fist caught Red on the bicep.

"Jasus, ma arse feels better already," smiled Po.

"Bet that's what ya said to your boyfriend last night," sniggered Red.

"Ya know, I remember the time a used ta like you."

"So, ya might go then, on Friday night?"

"That wee Kathleen's a doll."

"Is that a yes?"

"Are ya crazy, too right, I'm goin'."

"So am a back ta being your best friend, again," laughed Red.

"Well, let's say you're on probation."

"Oh, I see. It's like that, is it?"

Red turned and began walking back toward the doctors.

Po caught up with him and spun him around.

"Where are ya goin'?"

"I'm goin' back to the surgery to cancel the date with Kathleen. I only get dates for my best friends, and since you are not one a them . . . . ."

"But I am, I am. I am your best friend in the whole world, in the whole universe, so I am."

"I see. How good a friend?"

"The very, very best there is."

"Hmm."

"I am. I swear it."

"Hmm. So I can borrow your new radio for the weekend, then?"

"What?"

"Best friend."

"Ya, all right then. I suppose."

"By the way, ya do know those injections come in a group of three don't ya?"

"Piss off."

"Did he ask ya to come back next week?"

"Yeah."

"There ya go."

"I'm not goin' back then, no friggin' way."

"Not even ta see that 'wee doll' as ya call her?"

"Well, never thought of that."

"I have a feelin' ya might be getting a lot more health problems so a do."

"Come ta think of it, ma back has been very sore lately."

"There ya go, ah, sure as any man of the world will tell ya, sometimes love comes at a painful price."

End

The Great Sheep Caper

1960

The four boys were sitting on a granite, dry stone wall, overlooking Camlough Lake. It was a warm Saturday afternoon, and the soft cool breeze that brushed their faces was very welcome.

"Let's head down ta the lake," suggested Po.

"Do we have ta move?" complained the Bishop.

"Come on, lazy arse," said Red, as he pushed Bishop off the wall.

"There might be some birds down there skinny dippin'," commented Jumpy.

All three stopped and looked at him.

"Jumpy, you are one sad wee bastard," said Red.

"I heard they do it there, all the time," pleaded Jumpy.

"Yeah, right, of course they do," chipped in Bishop sarcastically.

"If ya ever get hung for being normal Jumpy, ya'll die an innocent man," smiled Po. This got him a round of applause and laughter.

They began making their way across the field, down the side of the valley towards the lake.

"Hi you, get outta this field. This is private property . . . out!" came a booming voice. The not so polite request came from a red-faced, grumpy looking farmer with a torn jacket, a flat cap that was probably worn by his great grandfather, and baggy stained trousers, held up by a thick cord tied around his waist.

"We're just goin' down to the lake, mister," answered Po.

"I don't give a shit where you're goin'. Go some other way and get outta my field."

The boys turned and went back up the field. When they reached where the farmer was standing, Po stopped. "We weren't doin' any harm, ya know mister."

"I don't give a shit. This is my land, see them sheep over there, they're mine. I own this land and I don't want you Newry bastards on it."

"I'm no bastard," snapped back Po. "At least my parents were married. I would doubt if yours were."

The farmer moved menacingly closer. His face now flushed with anger.

"Are ya sayin' my parents weren't married? Is that what you're sayin'?"

"Most likely brother and sister."

The farmer brought his stick down, hard, on Po's shoulder. As Po bent forward in pain he took a second blow across the back. Red moved forward fast and grabbed Po. The farmer had his stick in the air, ready to strike again. Red pushed Po toward Jumpy and Bishop, who grabbed him. Spinning around toward the farmer, Red's fist caught him just above his fat belly, in the solar plexus. He gasped and staggered and began running backwards, almost halfway down the field before he landed on his backside in a cow pat.

The boys didn't stop running until they reached Camlough village. Stopping to catch their breath, Bishop was the first to speak.

"What an auld bastard . . . ya'd think we were gonna steal his stupid sheep, or somethin'."

"Are ya ok, Po?" asked Red.

"No, I'm friggin', sore so I am."

Po removed his shirt to display two angry red marks on his white body.

"Look at what that bastard did, will ya?"

"Jasus, that looks sore," said Jumpy, touching the now swelling mark on Po's shoulder.

"For Christ's sake, Jumpy, why don't ya just test it with your fist? It's sore!"

"Sorry Po, it looks bad. What an auld bastard, but that was a great dig ya got at him, Red."

"And he landed in shit, too," laughed Po.

"I thought the way he was running backwards he'd go all the way ta the lake," added Jumpy.

The four laughed and giggled about the incident, all the way home.

Jumpy and Bishop said goodbye to Red and Po at Mill Street. The latter two walked up the hill towards home. Halfway up, Po stopped.

"I'm goin' ta get him, ya know."

"I had no doubt about it a'tall. I was wonderin' when ya would get around ta it."

"I think I might just have a way ta drive the auld frigger up the walls."

"What?"

"Naw, not yet. I haven't got it all in ma mind. I'll need to think about it a wee bit. I'll tell ya later tonight."

Later that night the gang was all gathered in Uncle Luigi's. The topic of conversation was the afternoon's events.

"He will be one sorry hay pitcher, for pickin' on me," smiled Po.

"What are ya goin' ta do, Po?" asked Bishop.

"I'm goin' ta teach him a lesson he won't forget in a hurry."

"What are ya goin' ta do?" asked Bishop again.

"Jumpy, doesn't your uncle have sheep out in Ballyholland?"

"Yeah, he has hundreds of them."

"Great stuff, now this is what I want ya ta do."

Po's voice dropped to a whisper as he instructed Jumpy. The others leaned forward to make sure they didn't miss anything.

On the way home, Red turned to Po.

"Ya know, I still don't understand what the frig you're gonna do?"

"Sure, ya'll enjoy it, I can bet on that. But he won't, a can tell ya."

That was all that Red could get out of him.

The following night Po had everyone standing around him at the same wall, where they had sat the day before. He had four cardboard boxes sitting on the ground, in front of him.

"Now this is what we're gonna do. The sheep are all in that wee shed or barn or whatever it's called, over there in the corner of the field. Grab one at a time and I will do the rest. And remember, no noise."

Eventually, the first sheep was grabbed and held for Po. As Red and Bishop held it, Po opened a box, took a cloth from his pocket and dipped it in the box. He then proceeded to smudge what was on the cloth onto the sheep's back. He repeated this three more times, dipping a new cloth in each of the boxes. This went on until all the sheep, of which there were fifteen, were done. Po collected up the boxes and they were all soon back on the road home to Newry.

About an hour later they were sitting in one of Uncle Luigi's snugs, drinking Coke.

"Well, come on, tell me what that was all about?" said Red, looking at Po.

Lowering his voice, Po leaned forward.

"Well now, ya see when a ram does the job on a ewe they have a sort of harness on him. The main part is on his chest, the harness is filled with a coloured dye ya see, and there is a part that releases a little of the dye when pressed. So every ewe he gets on, he marks their back ya see?"

"Yeah, go on."

"The farmer does the same every time a sheep is wormed or gets an injection so he knows what sheep have had what . . . ya understand?"

"I think I'm beginning ta get the picture," said Red, smiling.

"Tomorra, our friend at Camlough Lake will have sheep that have had every injection there is and have had a good time with the auld ram, as well."

Red raised his Coke bottle.

"Here's ta Camlough's first rainbow sheep."

"And, ta the auld bastard that owns them," added Po.

End

The Coke Bottle Race

1960

"Ok, now these are the rules, right?" said Anto.

"Right," came the unanimous reply.

"Now, we drop the Coke bottles off the stone bridge at Derrylecky, ok? No bets for the first mile. After that, even money for the next two miles. Then two ta one it will reach the Stone Bridge in Newry. To reach the sea I will give five ta one. Ya can bet on either bottle one or bottle two."

"Right, I'll have two bob on two not getting ta the Stone Bridge," said Jammy McAteer.

"Done."

They were all sitting around a table in Uncle Luigi's that Sunday afternoon. Anto was explaining his latest betting idea to all there. He was betting that an empty Coke bottle could make it all the way to the sea from the Derrylecky Bridge, which was six miles away. The agreement was that the bottle would be empty but re-capped; otherwise it would simply fill with water and sink.

Red and Po were walking along Hill Street when they met Topcoat.

"Were ya in Luigi's?" asked Po.

"Yeah, all the boys have left now. Anto was tellin' us about the Coke Bottle thing he is runnin'."

"He's goin' ta do it then? He was talkin' about it the other night," said Red.

"He's doing it later today so he is. I put on four bob my bottle would get ta Newry."

"Knowing Anto, I'm not too sure I would put a bet on this one."

"Well Red, I can tell ya it's all above board. We went over every single rule."

"So what happens, say, if one of the bottles gets stuck on an overhanging branch or somethin'?" asked Po.

"Ah, we covered that. We wait for exactly 15 minutes, then, if the bottle is still stuck, we take that as the end of the race for that bottle."

"Sounds like a good one ta me, maybe I will have a bet after all," said Red.

Later that day the whole gang were standing on the Derrylecky Bridge spanning the Clanrye River which at this point was about 20 feet wide and quite fast flowing.

Anto was standing in the middle of the bridge holding both Coke bottles in the air.

"As ya all can see, each bottle has its number clearly marked on the paper on the inside, so, are we all ready?"

"Yes," came the reply.

"I hereby declare the Great Coke Bottle Race open."

He dropped both bottles into the river to a great cheer from all there. The bridge soon cleared as everyone scrambled to the river banks to follow the progress of the bottles.

Two miles later, both bottles were intact and still moving with the river flow, although at one point one of the bottles seemed to get stuck. To roars of encouragement and a few swear words the bottle with great effort seemed to free itself and continue on its journey to the sea. As the river neared Newry it seemed to gather speed and the boys had at times to run to keep up. When the travelling group reached a small stone bridge at Carnbane, just a couple of miles from Newry, catastrophe stuck Coke bottle two as it smashed into a stone in the middle of the river ending its life with a loud bang and shattering of glass. This was a very emotional moment for some of the gang who had been following bottle two with great interest. The bottle had almost taken on a life of its own. There were some cheers, some swearing, some hat and cap removal and Jumpy Jones got a slap on the back of the head from Red as he was making the sign of the cross.

The Great Coke Bottle Race continued unabated along the swirling river, missing rocks, overhanging trees, even a cobble stoned weir. The cheering crowd continuing to urge, encourage, praise, and even in some cases pray for the little bottle as it bobbed on its way as if enjoying its short lived notoriety.

Suddenly, and without warning, the bottle snagged on something under the water about six feet from the bank. Everyone stopped. There was silence. The bottle spun, twisted, rolled, but was unable to free itself. Anto moved to the edge of the river bank beside Jumpy and Dunno McManus.
"How long?" asked Dunno.
"Six minutes," whispered Anto, almost to himself.
Anto bent over squinting to see if he could see what was holding the bottle. He stood up and turned to face Red and Po.
"I think it's a lost cause," he said sadly.
"No chance of it moving?" asked Red.
"Don't think so," answered Anto who seemed to be looking around.
"What's holding it?" asked Po.
"A friggin' big rock, it must be this size . . ." said Anto demonstrating the size with both arms outstretched. Somehow, during Anto's demonstration of rock size, his left hand hit Jumpy on the back. The force of the blow sent him forward, over the banks edge, screaming, into the River Clanrye. There was a great splash and, lo and behold, the waves caused by Jumpy's entry into the water, enabled the bottle to free itself and continue bobbing on its merry way to the cheers and roars of its new found fans. Jumpy was totally forgotten about and had to make his own way to the bank and scramble up to safety. Everyone was a hundred yards away by now, still cheering the bottle.

The bottle was now approaching perhaps the first really difficult part of the journey, under the Newry Town Hall, which stood proudly on a granite stone bridge. Jammed under the bridge were a myriad of rocks and other rubbish which could easily put an end to the bottles progress. However, the bottle moved to where the river flowed fastest and somehow missed the obstructions altogether.

"About a mile and a half now," smiled Anto at Red as they ran along Newry's Mall.

"Ya did that on purpose ya bastard."

"Did what?"

"Ya hit poor Jumpy on purpose."

"Me? Now Red, would I do such a terrible thing?"

"Without even thinking about it," replied Red.

"Maybe ya'r right, sure we'll never know will we. Sometimes things just happen, like as if God intended them to," said Anto looking up at the sky.

"Falsoni, you are so full of shit I'm surprised ya can even walk."

Anto's reply was a wry smile.

The Coke bottle duly made it all the way to Carlingford Lough and the sea. Some of the lads made money, most lost. Anto, it was said, made quite a bundle. The Great Coke Bottle Race is still talked about to this day. Debates still continue.

"It was fate."

"It was that bastard Anto."

"No, it was the bottle itself that did it."

"I think it was divine intervention."

"Divine intervention my arse."

Anto would just smile and walk away. Just on the off chance of the bottles making it to some exotic shore, he had placed notes inside. The now famous Coke bottle, commonly known as, Number One, contained the message, 'If found please return to Uncle Luigi's Café and Quality Ice Cream Parlour, Hill Street, Newry, Northern Ireland, Europe'.

Two years later Number One was indeed returned from a little village in Scotland called Ballantrae. It now has a place of honour in Uncle Luigi's Café admired by all its fans for its shear fortitude, strength and possible divine intervention.

End

Anto the Hero

1960

"I tell ya, she's the best lookin' bird in this town," said Anto.

"Aye, say's you, and like ya wouldn't be biased or anythin', would ya?" smiled Red.

"No way, sure all ya have ta do is look at her, she's friggin' perfect," continued Anto.

"Well sure, why don't ya ask her out then?" asked Po.

"She wouldn't go out with me in a month of Sundays, she's way too beautiful for the likes of me."

"That's a load a shit Anto. If she fancies ya, she'll go out with ya so she will," pointed out Red.

"I agree," chipped in Po.

"Look, for June O'Brian to go out with me, Jasus, I'd need ta be some kind of super hero or somethin'."

"Well, so be a super hero then," answered Po.

"Aye, right, just like that."

"Anto, how many way out strokes have we pulled off over the years between us, are ya sayin' we couldn't pull another one ta make ya a wonder man to June O'Brian?" continued Po.

"He's right Anto, we could set somethin' up that would work. Just needs a bit of plannin'," added Red.

"I wonder could we?" mused Anto.

"Why not, sure aren't we the best there is at set ups?" commented Red.

"Ya're right, we are the friggin' best. Ok, let's come up with somethin' then."

The planning had now begun in earnest. The task of making June O'Brian putty in Anto's hands was taken on by the three devious minds of Anto, Po and Red. It only took thirty minutes for Po to come up with a plan.

"Where does June work?" he asked.

"McCoy's in Monaghan Street, why?"

"And she would come home along the quay then?"

"Yeah, so?"

"Suppose someone had fallen into the canal, right? You happened ta be there and jumped in and saved him."

"No! no friggin' way, before ya ask," said Red.

"What?" asked Po.

"I'm just lettin' ya know up front, I'm not jumpin' into the friggin' canal ta help Anto's or anyone's else's love life."

"I never asked ya for Jasus sake, no, we use a dummy."

"Use Jumpy?" asked Anto.

"No, we use a real dummy, like the ones next door throw out all the time, what are they called? Mannequins, that's it."

"Ok, start from the beginning Po," said Anto.

Another half hour passed and the plan was complete. The whole thing was to be executed the very next day.

*   *   *

Red was standing on the canal bank looking down at the mannequin lying on the ground.

"Are ya sure the hair won't come off?"

"It won't, I stuck it on well and even put in a couple of screws," said Anto.

"Where did ya get the suit?"

"One of Uncle Luigi's. He was throwin' it out."

"Right, ok, so piss off then will ya and go and meet June comin' outta work."

The idea was that Anto would sort of accidentally run into June as she left work and walk along the quay with her. He would have a bag of breadcrumbs with him for the swans. He would ask June to help him with this. At the right moment Red and Po would throw the dummy into the water and begin shouting for help.

So far everything was working according to plan. Anto met June and was walking along the quay with her. They crossed the road to the canal bank and began feeding the swans. Just a little further down on the other side Red and Po were making ready.

"Right?" whispered Po.

"Right."

They threw the dummy into the canal causing a great splash.

"Help someone, help!" shouted both Po and Red.

"Oh my God, someone has fallen in," gasped June with her hands covering her mouth.

"Leave it ta me," replied a brave unflustered Anto.

He quickly stripped off his coat, shirt and shoes and dived into the canal. Swimming with some speed he headed towards the drowning man, now face down in the water.

"Well done Anto, you're very brave," shouted Po.

Red hit him in the ribs with his elbow.

"Will ya shut up ya friggin' ejit."

June was watching intently with her hands still covering her mouth. Anto had now reached the drowning man. He grabbed him and could be heard shouting, "Don't worry, I have ya, just relax, I have ya."

Anto had his arm around the drowning man's neck and using his free hand was swimming to the bank where Red and Po were waiting.

"Anto, ya friggin' ejit ya," shouted Red.

Anto stopped at the bank and looked up at his two mates.

"What?" he gasped.

"Look," said Po pointing, "Ya whorein' wally!"

Anto looked in the direction Po was pointing. The dummy was still floating in the water some ten feet away. Anto looked back up at the boys and then down at his arm. Under it he had a smiling dummies head! At the same time, June saw all this from the other side. She screamed, fainted and fell to the ground.

Later that evening as the three sat in Uncle Luigi's Café with heads in hands, Jumpy Jones arrived in an excited and talkative mood.

"Did ya hear, Jasus, ya won't believe this, wait till ya hear, they say a man with no head has been seen floating in the canal!"

All three looked up and answered together.

"Piss off."

End

The Kiss of Life

1960

"I have to get some money for the weekend or I'm in trouble," moaned Anto to Red and Po.

They were sitting in the first snug of Uncle Luigi's.

"What's so special about this weekend?" asked Po.

"I'm takin' Sally to Belfast on Saturday."

"Then ya will need some money for sure," said Red.

"Ya know, there's an idea I've been playin' with if ya will help me out Red?"

"Sure Anto, no problem. What is it?"

"Well, all ya have ta do is play dead."

"Play dead?" laughed Red.

"Simple as that. I want ya ta pretend ya are drowned when we're at the County River taday."

"What have ya planned?" asked Po.

"Ah, this is a beauty. I can't tell ya it all just yet, but will ya do it?"

"Ok, so, a have ta just pretend I've drowned in the water, right?"

"That's it, we'll pull ya out and all that, try First Aid and everythin' but nothin' works, ya have drowned."

"Sure, that sounds easy, it will scare the bejasus outta the boys."

"And, I'll give ya five bob for your part in it so a will."

45

"Five bob? Ya have a deal," smiled Red shaking Anto's hand.

Later that day the whole gang was at the County River. Some were in the water, others were just lying on the bank and the rest were playing football.

"Now are ya ready?" whispered Anto to Red.

"What do a do?"

"Dive in, pretend ya hit the bottom and just float to the top as if ya were drowned."

"I can't hold my friggin' breath for ever ya know, ya better be quick gettin' me out."

"Don't be worryin' about that, I'll be in the water beside ya."

"Ok, ya want me to go now?"

"Now would be good."

Red stood up and walked to the riverbank. He made a big deal about getting ready to dive in asking one of the lads how deep the water was at that spot. When he was ready, in he went. Anto and Po were directly behind him.

As per the plan, Po began to shout, "Somethin's happened ta Red, help, help!"

A number of the boys jumped in to help Po and Anto get Red out of the water. Red was playing his part well and not breathing. They got him onto the bank quickly and laid him on his back.

"What happened Anto?" asked Kitter Murray with concern in his voice.

"I think he might have hit the bottom," replied Anto lightly slapping Red's face.

"Is he all right?" asked Jumpy Jones.

"No, he has stopped breathin' so he has," replied Anto.

"What are ya goin' ta do?" continued Jumpy.

"Give Anto some room lads, he knows what he is doin'. He's done a First Aid course ya know," piped in Po.

Anto tilted Red's head back and opened his mouth. Leaning forward he placed his mouth over Red's and began the kiss of life. Red reacted immediately by pushing him away.

"Get off ya bastard."

"I was only givin' ya the kiss of life Red, to save ya," smiled Anto.

"Save someone else ya fruit," snorted Red sitting up rubbing his mouth and spitting.

Anto and Po by this time were in fits of laughter at Red's reaction. Somehow, Red did not see the funny side.

Later they were back in Uncle Luigi's Café sitting in the first snug.

"Well, sure that was easy wasn't it?" smiled Anto.

"What was easy, gettin' kissed by a fruit?" snapped Red.

"Here ya go ya sexy kisser, five bob as promised."

"Hold on a minute, what is this for exactly?"

"Gettin' drowned, sort of."

"What are ya talkin' about?"

"Look, didn't we have an agreement that if ya played drowned I would give ya five bob?"

"Yeah, but . . ."

"Well, ya did it, so here's your five bob."

"I don't get it, am I missin' somethin' here?"

Anto stood up to leave.

"No, ya did exactly as I wanted ya ta do."

"So, how did ya make money outta it then?" Red asked looking confused.

"Ah, well sure that was the genius bit ya see. I bet everyone I would get to kiss ya on the mouth before the day was out, and a did," Anto laughed as he began walking away.

"Ya low life, sneaky, bastard, fruit, whore . . ." Red shouted after him.

Anto didn't reply, he just smiled and waved his wallet.

"You knew about this didn't ya, ya wee bastard?" said Red now looking at a smiling Po.

"Not all of it, but sure ya have ta admit it was a good one."

"No it wasn't."

Po now stood up to leave, stopping as if he had thought of something.

"Can I ask ya a question Red, just between you and me?"

"What?"

Po bent forward and lowered his voice.

"Is Anto a good kisser?"

Po, luckily for his health and well being, made it out of Uncle Luigi's without being caught by Red.

End

The Christmas Present

1960

Red opened his front door to be greeted by the grinning face of his friend, Po.

"What the hell are ya doin' here so friggin' early?" mumbled Red, rubbing his eyes.

"It's Christmas Eve, ya lump," answered Po, as he pushed past Red and headed for the kitchen.

"So friggin' what?" shouted Red after him. Po never answered.

On entering the kitchen he found Red's mom and grandmother making breakfast.

"Look who's here, would ya?" said Granny Morgan, smiling at Po.

"I think he can smell food a mile away," answered Red's mom, Jean.

"Well, ya see, your generosity and cookin' skills in the breakfast department are known throughout Ireland," smiled Po.

"Aye, right. Sit yourself down there, if ya want some breakfast," smiled Granny Morgan.

"Sit you down there, too, young man," said Granny, looking at Red.

After polishing off two eggs, two slims (potato bread), fried tomatoes, fried soda bread, black pudding, two sausages and two mugs of tea, Po sat back and patted his tummy.

"Ya should be cooking for the Queen, so ya should. That was fantastic," smiled Po.

"Would ya listen to your man with his silver tongue, would ya?" smiled Granny Morgan.

"What did ya get your parents for Christmas?" asked Jean.

"I got ma da a lovely scarf and a tie. And a got me mom an apron and a nice headscarf."

"That's nice. What are ya doin' up so early, anyway?" asked Jean.

"I have a couple of presents ta get yet, and himself has promised ta help me pick them."

"Yeah, he has ta get somethin' nice for the love of his life to impress her, ya see," sneered Red.

"Oh, ya have a girl on the go, have ya?" said Granny Morgan, smiling.

Po blushed and looked down at his knees.

"Don't be listenin' ta that ejit, for God's sake," he mumbled.

"He's datin' your wee one, Trish O'Hagan, from Chinatown, so he is," smiled Red.

Red felt the sharp pain travel up his leg, as Po's shoe caught him on the ankle bone with some force, under the table.

"Oh, I know the O'Hagans. Nice family, so they are," said Jean, clearing the table.

When Jean and Granny Morgan were out of hearing, Po stood up and grabbed Red by the sleeve.

"Come on you, will ya, a want to get this present today ya know."

"Jasus, will ya let me finish ma breakfast, will ya, 'Posie Wosie'."

Po pulled Red out of the chair.

"Ya finished ten minutes ago, ya slabber. Come on."

Red gave in, got his coat, and the two headed off towards the centre of town.

"Have ya anything in mind to buy wee Trish?"

"No idea a'tall, creep."

"How about one of them wee trainin' bras?"

"What the frig are ya talking about? Trish has great yokes, so she has."

"An how would you know?"

"I just know, is all."

"Well, I heard different."

"What did ya hear?" snapped Po, stopping and pulling Red around by the shoulder.

"Well . . . ." said Red, rubbing his chin. "The word is, ya tried ta grope her one night, and missed!"

Red took off at speed before Po's fist could make contact.

*   *   *

"Ok, we are narrowed down ta what?" asked Red.

Both stopped off at Uncle Luigi's for a Coke to discuss what type of present Po should buy. Po looked down at the scribbled list on the table.

"A necklace, a watch, or a ring."

"How's it goin'?" came the voice of Anto, as he leaned across the counter, towel draped over his shoulder and wearing a well-stained, white apron.

"Don't ask," sneered Red.

"Why don't ya get her a bit, then?" asked Anto, as he began to move away.

"A bit of what?" asked Po, innocently.

"Well, from what I hear, she is very fond of a bit . . ." said Anto disappearing.

"He's a bastard, a whore, and a pismire, ya know," said Po, seriously to Red.

"I know, I know," said Red, fighting to keep his face straight.

"Ok, so what about the watch, then?"

"Naw, bad idea. I'm sure she already has a watch, so it's not somethin' she would need, is it?" Red pointed out.

"Never thought a that, right enough."

"So how about a gold bracelet, then?"

"Are ya out of your friggin' mind? Do ya know how much them things cost?"

"Ahhh, but genius here knows how ta get one very cheap."

"Serious?"

"Serious. How much de ya want ta spend on her?"

"A reckon about a fiver."

"That would do it, ok."

"Will ya tell me, ya dick. Will ya?"

"Now hold on, my wee Trish lover, till a think . . . . .yeah, that would work ok."

"What, what?"

"A would need another Coke ta get the plan settled in ma head, ya see."

"Shithead," mumbled Po, getting out of the snug.

"One has ta have sustenance for the thinkin' process, ya know."
"Jasus, I'm surrounded by bastards and whores," mumbled Po, as he left for the counter.

"Ok, ya have your Coke, what's your idea?"
"John."
"John?"
"Yeah, John."
"John, John, John who?"
"John, in the Pawn."
"What?"
"Ya would pay a lot more that a fiver for a good bracelet, right? We can get one in the pawn, a second-hand one, for a few quid. My granny has this stuff for bringing up gold like brand new. We get a new box for the bracelet from one of the jewellers, and you're home free."
"It'll work, for sure. You're nothin' short of a friggin' genius, Morgan."
"Will ya tell me something I don't know, will ya?" said Red, blowing his fingernails.

The two arrived at the pawn shop on Hill Street and were served by the boss, himself, John. He was a man in his 60's, slightly hunched, with an ill-fitting, very obvious, very bad wig.
"So it's a bracelet ya want, is it, young man?" asked John.
John produced a tray of bracelets and the boys inspected them closely.
"That one looks nice," said Po, pointing to a chain link bracelet.
"Ah, ya have a good eye, so ya have. Unusual link in that one. Ya'll not see one of them around here, for sure."
"How much is it?" asked Red.
John rubbed his chin.
"Well, due to the fact that it is, as a said, unusual, I could let ya have it for say four pounds and I would be giving it away at that."
Po was about to accept the deal when he felt Red's knee in his thigh.
"Would like that one for sure, but it is more than we can afford, sorry," said Red, pulling Po away from the counter.
"Hold on a minute, now. Since its Christmas, tell ya what I'll do . . . . let's see, I could let ya have it for . . . three pounds fifteen shillings. How's that?" said John.
"That's really good of ya, John, but ya see, all we have ta spend is three pounds ten shillings," said Red, innocently.

John rubbed his face in his hands.

"Yis ought ta be ashamed of yourselves, robbing a poor businessman at Christmas. Go on then, three pounds ten shillings it is."

The bracelet was in Po's pocket when he went to one of the town jewellers, where he knew one of the girls that worked there and got a box for nothing. From there it was straight to Red's house for Granny Morgan's magic gold cleaner. In a very short time they had the bracelet gleaming, boxed and wrapped with a blue ribbon tied in a bow.

"A ribbon?" exclaimed Red.

"Yeah, what's wrong with that?"

"Nothin'."

"What's wrong with it?"

"Bit . . . sissy."

"Would ya ever piss off? Ya have no taste a'tall, Morgan."

The two ended back in Luigi's. Anto joined them and Po related to him, in detail, the morning's events.

"Ya did well there, Po. It was a good idea, and, saved ya a fortune, as well," commented Anto, as he got up to go back to work. A few feet away from the snug, he stopped and returned with a great grin across his face.

"Ya know, a just thought of somethin'. Did ya ever think?" Anto burst out laughing at his idea. "Did . . . ya . . . ever think, maybe it was Trish that pawned the thing in the first place . . ."

Red and Po exchanged glances, both looking sombre.

The colour had totally left Po's face as he spoke in a low voice.

"Jasus Christ, I never thought a that!"

"You've no choice at this stage, ya'll just have ta give it to her," said Red, seriously.

On Boxing Day, Red, Anto and a few of the gang were sitting in the first snug in Uncle Luigi's, drinking coffee and discussing what presents they got for Christmas, and what presents they bought. Po arrived and ordered a Coke. He motioned to Red to go to another snug. When they were settled Red asked if the bracelet was liked by Po's girlfriend.

"Jasus, I nearly shit so a did."

"What, she didn't like it?" asked Red.

"That wasn't the problem. She friggin' loved it, so she did."

"What are ya talkin' about, for Christ's sake? You've lost me."

"Well, I gave her the box and she was all smiles. She opened it and her face lit up. 'Oh my God Po, it is beautiful, just beautiful. The bestest present I ever got,' she said. I tell ya, she was almost in tears, so she was."

"Brilliant, it was a success, then," smiled Red, patting Po on the shoulder.

"That it was, but there was a minute there when I thought I was in shit."

"Why?"

"Well, she put it on and was admiring it when she suddenly stopped and stared at it. She began to examine it closely. That's when a started ta panic," said Po, as he paused to sip his Coke.

"Well, well?" asked Red, impatiently.

"Well, she suddenly smiled from ear ta ear and says, 'This is even better'."

"Even better? What was she talkin' about?"

"Will ya wait? Do ya know, ya have no patience a'tall. Do ya know that?"

"Will ya tell me, ya wee rat, or I'll poke your eyes out."

"Aye, aye," laughed Po.

"Smart wee bugger."

"Well, anyway, as a was sayin', she started smilin' and said, 'My cousin Margaret will be green with envy.' So, a asked why?"

Po paused for another long sip of his Coke, only to be interrupted by a slap on the head from Red.

"Will ya piss off, will ya," said an indignant Po, rubbing his head.

"Will ya, for frig sake, get on with it?"

"Well, she says, 'Ma cousin Margaret had a bracelet exactly the same as this. She was always sticking it in ma face ta show off'."

"Oh no, Jasus . . . she recognised it?" asked Red, intently.

"Wait ta ya hear the story. Her cousin Margaret, who was, I heard, the biggest snob ever to wear knickers, needed money for somethin' or other and only pawned the bracelet, so she did, never renewed it, and lost it."

"Jasus! And this was your one's bracelet, then?"

"This was the very bracelet. Remember what John in the Pawn said, that it was unusual, that there wouldn't be another one around these parts?"

"I remember, all right. Shit, that was a close call, all right."

"She says she will be stickin' it in her cousin's face from now on and will enjoy it."

"Wow, ya must have been havin' kittens."

"It was touch and go there for a bit, I tell ya, a was sweatin', all right."

"So all's rosy in the garden, I suppose. Ya got a wee kiss and almost a wee grope, did ya?"

"Mind your own business."

Red laughed and slapped Po on the shoulder.

"All's well that ends well, right?"

"That was the problem ya see. It didn't end just yet."

"There's more?"

"Well a was thinkin', what if the cousin Margaret had a secret mark or somethin' on the bracelet, in case it was stolen or somethin'?"

"Jasus! Never thought a that."

"Well as it happens, didn't she only run into the snobby cousin, accidentally-on-purpose last night."

"And?"

"She shows her the bracelet. The cousin says, 'It's a lovely bracelet Trish, very like one I had, but mine was a bit more expensive, I would say'."

"Snobby bitch."

"My very own thoughts. But sure your one, Trish, is no dumb-dumb, ya know."

"What did she say?"

"Well Margaret, I suppose your bracelet might have cost a couple of pennies more, dependin' on where it was bought. But the point is, my beautiful bracelet is on my arm for all to see. Where is your expensive one?"

"I'd bet that was the end of the conversation," laughed Red.

"It was, for sure. Margaret turned and marched off with her head in the air. When a talked ta Trish this mornin' she said it was the first time in her life she ever got one over on the snobby cousin. She was just delighted."

"Wow, what a story. Brilliant. The sad thing for us is we can never tell anyone," laughed Red.

"A know, but a came up with somethin' a am goin' ta tell Trish ta say to your one if she gets any more grief from her."

"What's that?" asked Red.

"She who gets and throws away, lives to regret another day."

They both laughed and clinked their Coke bottles.

Christmas is a time for giving, a time for joy and laughter, a time for being inventive when choosing presents, a time for, sometimes, stretching the truth . . . just a tiny little bit!

End

The Class Project

1960

Red and Po were in deep discussion, with Jumpy, Dunno, Ginger and the Bishop, in the back garden of Red's house, on Castle Street.

"Wait a minute. What he wants is ways to raise money ta help the black babies, isn't it?" asked Bishop.

"Look, this is what he said. He wants us ta come up with ideas for Newry people to help the starving black babies in Africa. That's the friggin' project," commented Ginger.

"So what do we do, then?" asked Po. "Have ya any ideas, Red?"

"Well, as I see it, we have ta come up with ideas for Newry people ta help the starvin' black babies in Africa."

"You're such a smart mouth, Morgan. Seriously, what will we do?"

"Well, we need ta think of who actually has money and how we can get them to give it ta the starvin'," said Ginger.

"Ginger's right. So who do we know has loads of money, then?" asked Red.

"Joe Connor," said Jumpy.

"Joe Connor, the butcher?" asked Red.

"Yeah, he's loaded."

"Will someone hit him on the head with a heavy log," said Red.

"We need an organisation with lots of money to help the whole country," Red went on.

The boys were gathered to discuss a class project given to them by their Religious Education Teacher, Mr. Reed. They were asked to get into groups of six and then to go off and come back in one week with a completed paper on how Newry people could best raise money to help the black babies in Africa. Mr. Reed emphasised that one pound could save a child's life for a year.

"Like, do ya mean a big business?" asked Dunno.

"That's it, Dunno. A big friggin' loaded-with-money business, or a group of people doin' somethin' to raise the money," replied Red.

"What about the government?" asked Bishop.

"The government gives thousands of pounds anyway, but we should list them," said Po, writing on his jotter.

"Jasus, a got it. A friggin' got it," exclaimed Red, excitedly.

"Who?" asked Po.

"The friggin' church."

"The church?" asked Po.

"Yeah, the friggin' church."

"De ya mean like, the Cathedral, Red?" asked Dunno.

"The Catholic Church . . . . yes!" said Red, enthusiastically.

"The very ones, of course," put in Po.

"Have they money?" asked Bishop.

"Are ya serious? Of course they have, millions and millions."

"Come ta think of it, I suppose they do, right enough," added Bishop.

"Ok, this is the way ta go, a can see it clear now," said Red.

"So, what are ya thinkin', that we ask the church for money?" asked Jumpy.

"Don't be stupid Jumpy. The church doesn't give money ta charity."

"Of course they do. Don't they send missionaries and all that stuff ta Africa?"

"Missionaries are sort of like Catholic Church recruiters. It's their job ta get more converts than the protestants."

"Ok, got ya . . . but don't they give money ta help the starvin'?"

"Are ya out of your head? When was the last time ya heard of the church givin' away anythin'? Yeah, they give money ta the poor all right, but it's not their money. It's my ma and da's money and your ma and da's money, not the church's money," commented Bishop.

"You're on the ball, Bishop," laughed Red.

"Well, this doesn't make sense," mumbled Jumpy.

"What doesn't make sense, Jumpy?" asked Red.

"Well, if it's as Bishop says, and the church don't give money ta the poor, what's the point of listin' them?"

"He's right," added Ginger.

"Well, if we can show the church how ta save some money in the Newry area, then with the money they save, they give ta the black babies. That way, they are not losin' anythin', are they?" said Red.

"Sound's good ta me," commented Bishop.

"Me too," added Dunno.

"Ok, so what's the church's biggest expense?" asked Red.

"The Cathedral?" suggested Po.

"Good one, write that down," said Red.

"I know, the Bishop's Palace up there on the Armagh Road," commented Jumpy.

"Good one Jumpy, that must cost a fortune ta run," replied Red.

"So how do we start and go about gettin' the figures and stuff?" asked Po.

"I think we should divide it into individual jobs. We can do it in pairs."

"Brilliant. Po's with me. Bishop, you team up with Ginger. And that will leave the brains of the outfit Jumpy and Dunno together," laughed Red.

"Ha ha," sneered Jumpy.

They each got their assignments. Red and Po were to look into ways of saving money at the Bishop's Palace. Bishop and Ginger decided to look at priests' fees for masses and weddings, etc. And Jumpy and Dunno were to look into church-sponsored activities, like Dances and Record Hops, etc., to raise money. The School Project, or as they saw it, the adventure, had begun. The week was packed with industrious, non-stop activity by the team. They finally got all their notes together for Bishop, who, being the best writer, got it all down neatly on paper. Their project was handed in to Mr. Reed next day and they were told the papers would be marked and returned to them at the next class, three days later.

*   *   *

Class 3C were in the Woodwork room when a Prefect came in and gave a message to Mr. Haig.

"Ok, Morgan, Hillen, Jones, McVerry, McManus and Keenan, stop what you are doing and go to the Principal's Office now, please."

The group swapped glances, shrugged shoulders and did what they were told. On arrival at the Principal's Office, Red knocked the door and opened it. The school Secretary, Miss Courtney, was seated at her desk. She looked up.

"Ah, Mr. Morgan. Are the rest there with you?"

"Yes Miss."

"Ok, take a seat outside until you are called."

"Yes Miss."

They all sat down and began to question, in whispers, the reason for being there.

Five minutes later the door opened and Miss Courtney came out, holding some envelopes.

"Now boys, the Principal wants you to give these to your parents, please." She handed one to each of them.

"Ok, you may go back to your class, now."

On the way back to the Woodwork Class Po was the first to speak.

"I'm gonna open this, now."

"No, not now, Po. Wait till after school so we will be able ta close it again without it being noticed," said Red.

It was so agreed and after school they all arrived at Red's house where Red held his envelope over a steaming kettle until the flap was loose enough to open. They all went into the back garden and Red began to read the letter out loud.

Dear Mr. and Mrs. Morgan,

The Principal, Mr. Ferron, requires you to attend an urgent meeting on Friday afternoon at 3.30pm in the school Assembly Hall, regarding a very serious matter involving your son. .

Miss P.R. Courtney
Secretary.

"Jasus, this sounds serious. What's it about?" asked Red, to no one in particular.

"Did any of yis do anythin'?" asked Bishop.

"No, don't think so," was the general comment.

"Somebody must a done somethin'," said Po.

"No, it's not that a'tall, Po," said Red, looking at the letter.

"Huh?"

"Think about it. If you, or Bishop, or me, did anythin' we would get called ta the Principal's Office, right? Not all of us. This has ta do with our project. It is the only thing we were all involved in, together."

"He's right. That's what it has ta be," commented Ginger.

"But we finished it, so we did, and ya said yourself it was great," said Dunno.

"It was great, so it was," said Red.

"Shit, this sounds like big trouble," said Jumpy.

*   *   *

Vinnie Morgan, Red's father, was talking to Sean Hillen as they waited for the Principal in the Assembly Hall.

"None of the boys seem ta know what's goin' on, and I am inclined ta believe them. I know when I am being lied to, for sure," said Vinnie.

"I questioned my fella about it, and he seem ta be at a loss, as well."

"Good afternoon, ladies and gentlemen," came the booming voice of Mr. Ferron, as he entered the hall with the school Chaplin, Father Meed, and the Secretary, Miss Courtney.

"Now, first of all, may I thank you all for coming, and indeed, Father Meed, also. Now, ladies and gentleman, we are at this time faced with a very, very serious problem. This problem has presented itself in the form of a class project given to your sons by Mr. Reed, last week. It appears the class was asked to, in groups of six, come up with ideas in which the people of Newry could, in some way, raise money that would help the poor unfortunate children and their families in Africa."

"God and His Holy Mother bless them," said Father Meed, making the sign of the cross.

"Hear, hear," agreed everyone, blessing themselves.

"Well, to continue, your sons handed in their report to Mr. Reed, who, may I say, was so shocked and concerned, that he came straight to me. He was, I can tell you, quite upset. He informed me of the, may I say, disgraceful contents your sons handed in as their Project. Having read the document, I agreed with Mr. Reed, and at that time thought it appropriate to bring in Father Meed, who was, may I add, also shocked and outraged at what he read. I have here copies of the said project which will be distributed to you, so you may read for yourselves."

The papers were distributed and the parents began reading the cause of all the problems.

Class 3C Project:
Group 4: Morgan, Hillen, McAteer, Jones, Keenan, McManus.

How People and Groups in the Newry Area can Help the Starving
People of Africa.

The Church

1. That Bishop, Dr. O'Docherty, sell his Palace and grounds on the Armagh Road for the estimated value of £3,700,000, and move into the Parochial House.
2. Having then no need for a full time gardener, also saving an estimated £2,600 per year.
3. That the Bishop walk, or cycle to mass on Sundays and sell his limo for an estimated £7,000.
4. That he let his driver go, saving an estimated £2,600 per year.
5. That the Bishop learn to cook therefore no longer needing a chef, saving an estimated £3,420 per year.
6. That the priests give up 10% of their earnings from Masses, Weddings, Funerals, Death Offerings, Baptisms, etc, estimated (for 10 priests) at £140,000 each, making a total of £1,400 per week, making £728,000 for the fund, per year.
7. That the priests run a Record Hop every Wednesday and give the estimated proceeds of £1,500 to the fund making £78,000 per year.
8. That the priests give up 10% of the proceeds of the Saturday and Sunday night dances, estimated to be £1,400 to the fund making £72,800.

We believe the above would raise a total of **£4,587,220**

This, in the first year, would save the lives of: **4,587,220** children.

PS: We would also like to add, that if the above ideas were followed in 50 towns in Ireland, not including the selling of property or letting staff go, just implementing sections 6 and 7, it would raise enough money to save the lives of:

43 Million Children

There was silence. Father Meed stood up and cleared his throat.

"As you can all see, this is a total disgrace. It is, to say the least, disrespectful to the Bishop, the priests, in fact, Mother Church herself, and cannot, and will not, be tolerated," Father Meed sat down.

Mr. Ferron now took the floor.

"This is a very serious matter and I must inform you that the school is now considering expelling the six boys concerned."

Bishop Keenan's father put up his hand and stood up.

"Now, I don't know about the rest of the parents, but I don't see what all the fuss is about, to be honest. The lads were just giving an opinion, which I would hope they are allowed to do."

"I would totally agree with that," said Red's father, standing.

"My son gave an opinion that if certain changes were made, money would be saved, which could save the lives of many 1000's of starving children. What is wrong with that?"

There was a chorus of 'hear hears' around the parents.

Father Meed stood up. His face was bright red.

"That is not the point. How dare school children criticize the church, or the men of God that serve her. This will not be allowed. This, so called report, handed in by these boys, is nothing less than a big joke to them. They are making fun of God's Church. This is nothing less than sacrilege."

"So, you are saying, Father, that our boys could be expelled for this report?" asked Po's father.

"It is very possible they will," said Father Meed, angrily.

Red's father stood up and spoke to Mr. Ferron.

"Would it be possible for the parents to have five minutes to discuss this and give you our agreed opinion?"

"That would be fine."

The boys' parents went off to a corner of the room and began a huddled discussion.

The boys, too, put their heads together and had a discussion.

Five minutes later the parents returned to their seats and Mr. Keenan stood up.

"It is our agreed opinion that the boys were not making a joke of the church and were, in fact, simply giving their combined opinion on how to raise money for a worthy cause. We further think that expelling these boys would be a great injustice."

"We will take your answer under advisement and you will receive our decision by letter within the next seven days," said Mr Ferron, in a very official tone.

Red Morgan stood up.

"Sir, may I say something?"

"I think you have said quite enough already, young man," growled Mr. Ferron.

"Let the boys have their say," commented Mr. Jones.

A chorus of agreement followed from all the parents. Mr. Ferron looked at Father Meed, who held his hands up in an expression of 'might as well'.

"Ok, Morgan, what have you got to say?"

"I have been asked ta speak on behalf of all the boys, here. Having read what we handed in again, and listened to what you and Father Meed had ta say, I just have one thing ta ask. Are you both sayin', yourself, on behalf of the school, and Father Meed on behalf a the church, that in your opinion we are totally wrong and that in your opinion, prestige is far more important than life? This is how it will be seen by the people of Newry and the newspapers, as well."

Red sat down to a round of applause from everyone. That is, of course, with the exception of Father Meed and Mr. Ferron. The parents were told once again that they would be contacted by letter within a few days.

Red's father stopped on the way home and turned Red to face him.

"I am very proud of you and of the other boys for what ya did. I agree with everythin' ya said, as do the other parents. It is time that fat Bishop, his Lardship, was told what was what. I wonder if they will tell him?" he laughed, loudly. "I, somehow or other, don't think they will, and if ya tell your mother I called him Lardship I will kill you slowly and bury your body where it will never be found."

A week later, they all got their letters from the headmaster who informed them that no further action would be taken on the matter.

"Ya heard, then?" asked Po, as he met Red on Hill Street.

"Yeah."

"And?"

"And what?"

"What'd ya think?"

"I think they had no choice. When we mentioned the newspapers it scared the shit outta them."

"I think you're right," laughed Po. "Mentioning the newspapers was a great idea."

"That it was."

"Ya know, a had another idea."

"I'm afraid ta ask," laughed Red.

"Did ya ever see a skinny Bishop?"

"Very few. Why?"

"De ya remember that thing we did in class one time, about how ta work out a person's ideal weight by their height and build?"

"Yeah, I remember."

"Well, what we do is, find out the correct weight for all the Bishops in Ireland. For every pound overweight they are, they have to donate . . . say £5 to the fund."

Red laughed, loudly. "Save the starving in Africa? That would save the starving of the world."

End

Excuse Me Sir

1960

"Excuse me, Sir. Are you collecting for the black babies in Africa?" asked Anto, as he caught up with the dark figure walking slowly up Mill Street.

"As a matter of fact, I am. Would you like to make a contribution?"

"Yes, I might."

"That's very kind of you, Sir."

"I know. Part of my nature, an how much would ya be lookin'?"

"Well, lookin' at you, it's easy ta see you are a man of means, and of good breeding. So I think five pounds would be just perfect."

"That's a lot of money."

"That it is, but think of all the good it would do."

"There is that, I suppose. Now if I were to give ya five pounds, what, exactly, would ya do with it?"

"Well, as I said, Sir, it would do a lot of good, I can assure you. Provide inner sustenance, liquid refreshments, entertainment, and of course, grateful thanks from one who has, and knows sufferin'."

"Ya have suffered, your own self, then?"

"Indeed I have, Sir. Mental, emotional, and physical pain beyond belief."

"Wow, that is awful. I am sorry ta hear that."

"Thank you for your kind words, Sir."

"Yo," came the voice of Po, crossing the street.

"If it isn't fartface," smiled Anto.

"Where yis goin'?" asked Po.

"With the dark fella, here."

"Jasus, would ya look at the state of him," laughed Po.

"I did four chimneys this morning, with me grandda so a did, what de ya expect ma ta look like?" grumbled Red.

"Sure, aren't ya the great wee chimney sweep, altogether?" laughed Po.

"Sure, I didn't recognise him a'tall, Po. I thought he was one of them missionaries from Africa collectin' for the black babies. I'm glad ya came along. He almost had a fiver off me," laughed Anto.

"Aren't yous, two, very funny, altogether?" snarled Red.

"Here, let me ask ya a question, Red. When you're helpin' your grandda clean the chimneys, does the soot get under your clothes?" asked Anto.

"Sometimes. Why?"

"Hmm, interestin'," mused Anto, rubbing his chin. "And a bet it's a bitch to get it all off."

"Why are ya so interested in soot, all of a sudden?" asked Red, stopping and looking at him.

"Sure, can a mate not ask an innocent question?" said Po, seriously.

"Why don't ya back him up, Po?" snapped Red.

"Isn't it terrible Anto, the abuse and insults ya get for just askin' a friend a simple question?"

"Terrible? I would say it's worse than that. I would call it atrocious."

"Wow! Sure, that's a great word. Where did ya get it?" asked Po, seriously.

"Was in the 'Hotspur'. Last week's issue."

"Must remember it."

"Will yous two piss away off? I'm goin' home for ma dinner," complained Red.

"I was just wonderin' if your willie gets all black?" said Anto.

"Are ya indeed. Would ya like to see?"

"Jasus, no! Sure, I'm just after ma dinner," pleaded Anto.

"Are ya goin' out tonight?" asked Po.

"I have a date with Maureen. Why?"

"Christ, Anto, it could be a new book," exclaimed Po.

"A new book?" said Anto.

"Yeah. Ya remember 'Have Gun Will Travel'?"

"Yeah."

"This one could be, 'Black Willie Will Travel'."

"Brilliant! Would be great. I'd buy that, so a would," laughed Anto.

"Jasus, yis are so funny. If it wasn't for the fact that yis are sufferin' from mental defects, a would die laughin'."

"But ya'll have ta make sure your willie is scrubbed clean for tonight, ya know," smiled Po.

"That he will, Po. Sure, what would happen if Maureen were ta take hold of it? If she could find it, that is. She'd be covered in soot," laughed Anto.

"Are there many Chimney Sweeps in Newry Red? Seriously, now," asked Po.

"Why?"

"Well, sure, ya could start the 'Black Willie Club'."

Some fifty yards down the street Red stopped to catch his breath. Po was too fast for him.

"I'll get ya later, ya wee shit," shouted Red after him.

Po shouted back, "Confucious say, 'Man with black willie should not threaten good lookin' man with white willie or he will become black willieless man'."

Two days later, Po had arranged to meet Red to play football. He called to Red's house and was directed by Granny Morgan to the back yard, where Red was. He soon spotted him digging in the vegetable garden.

"Well, shitface?" smiled Po.

"If it isn't dickhead," answered Red.

"What are ya doin'?"

"Just clearing a spot for grandda. He's puttin' in some cabbage."

"Yo," came the voice of Anto, walking towards them.

"Well, what's the craic?" said Po, as Anto arrived beside him.

"Ask him. He asked me ta call at this time, for some reason," replied Anto, nodding towards Red.

"Yeah, wanted ta show ya something. Just be a minute," answered Red.

"Po, will ya go into the hen house and go through the straw, an' see if there are any eggs?" continued Red.

"No problem. You're talkin' ta the leadin' egg finder in Newry."

"I just need to throw some stuff onto the roof ta get it out of the way."

Red winked at Anto who had developed a puzzled look on his face.

Po went into the hen house and began his search through the straw for eggs. Red climbed onto the roof where a lot of junk was stored. He pulled a large bag to the edge.

"Po, did ya get any?" shouted Red.

"Not yet," came the reply.

"It's ok. Just leave it for now. We can look later," replied Red.

Po emerged from the hen house just in time to have a large bag of soot tipped on top of him. He was totally covered, from head to toe.

"Friggin', bastardin', whorein' shitmire, so ya are, Morgan," screamed Po coughing and sneezing.

Anto was bent over, laughing loudly as Red jumped down from the roof.

"Now, ya wee frigger, ya remember your wee Confucious sayin' the other day. Well, I have one, too. 'Confucious say, he who mocks man with black willie liable to have honourable blackout'."

End

The Glar Crossing

1960

Carlingford Lough, one of Ireland's most beautiful areas, comes up to within a couple of miles of Newry Town centre. When the tide goes out, it leaves behind deep black, sticky, foul-smelling sediment which has a top layer of glistening silver. This is known locally as 'glar'.

"It's not that friggin' funny, Morgan!" mumbled Anto.
Red, and Anto were sitting in the first snug of Uncle Luigi's, drinking coffee.
"I know, Anto, sure ma heart bleeds for ya so it does," Red burst out laughing, again.
"Bastard! You and that Hillen bugger were tarred with the same brush."
"Ok, now let me get this straight. He put a plastic bucket of all the slops he could find on top a the backyard door, right? He calls ya to come quick, ya do, and get the whole shit on your head?"
"That's it."
"Jasus," said Red, trying hard not to laugh again.
"But de ya want ta hear the real funny bit?"
"Can't wait."
"Ya remember that cord jacket ya lent me? Well, I was wearin' it," now it was Anto's turn to laugh.

There was silence, then Red spoke, almost in a whisper.

"My cord jacket, the new brown one, that I loaned ya after ya begged me for two days, was covered in slops? Tell me you're windin' me up, Anto."

"I was goin' out, so a was at the time. Sure, it wasn't my fault," pleaded Anto with his arms outstretched.

"I am tellin' ya, Po Hillen is goin' ta die, slowly."

*　　*　　*

Red was feeding his grandmother's chickens and being followed around the yard by Po.

"Look, sure didn't a get it all Dry Cleaned for ya. It looks as good as new, even better."

"Right, right, right, a heard ya the first time."

"Am a all forgiven? Give us a kiss then."

"Ya come one step closer Hillen and ya'll get that spade across your head so ya will."

Po giggled. "Ok then, so what do ya think of ma idea then?"

"Stupid."

"Look, all we need is about 6 planks, am tellin' ya," explained Po.

"I can hear what you're tellin' me clearly, Po. What I'm sayin' is it won't work."

"Of course it will. I tried out a wee plank on it last week and I could stand on it, so I could."

"Well, go for it, then. If ya want ta take the risk I'm not goin' ta stop ya," said Red, dryly.

"But a need ya ta give me a hand with the planks."

"Sure, I'll give ya a hand but I'm not walkin' across them, I can tell ya now."

"You're a cowardly custard, a yellow belly, a . . ."

"I know, a wee girl's trainin' bra. But I'm still not walkin' across that glar, ya can call me what ya like."

"All right then Miss Morgan, I'll call for ya later, if you're not playin' with your dolls."

Red's answer was just two fingers.

After Po had left, Red suddenly stood bolt upright and smiled. 'No need ta kill the wee whore, sufferin' is much better,' he thought.

*　　*　　*

Red arrived at Uncle Luigi's, went around the counter and called Anto, who was working out back. He explained his idea in detail to Anto, who was giggling, jumping up and down, and, in general, enjoying every word that came out of Red's mouth.

"Ah Jasus, sure that's brilliant! A can't wait," laughed Anto.

"Now, not a word ta any of the lads either, ok?"

"Ok."

That afternoon Po arrived at Red's house with Dunno and Ginger who he had coerced into helping him carry a number of planks from his back garden.

"Anto's meetin' us down there," said Po, as Red arrived at his front door.

"Are these the planks you're goin' ta use?" asked Red.

"Yeah, I took a couple extra, just in case."

"They're not very wide, are they?" said Red, examining the planks.

"They're wide enough, for Jasus' sake. Sure they only have to be the width of ma foot, don't they?"

"If ya say so."

Ten minutes later they arrived at the middle bank, just past the large metal railway bridge. Po wanted to put some planks across from the middle bank to the canal bank, on the other side. The reason for this, well, that was anyone's guess. When asked, Po would simply say, "No one's done it before. It'll be history."

When they reached the spot Po had in mind they found Anto sitting on the bank, waiting. After the grunted greetings were finished with, Po set about his plan.

"Now it's very important to lay the planks down very carefully. Otherwise they will just sink into the glar," explained Po.

"How many planks will it take, Po?" asked Anto.

"I would say ten should do it. But what I'm goin' ta do is lay them in twos, one beside the other."

The great plank bridge had begun. Po walked along the first two planks after they were laid side by side to test them and was delighted to report to all there that they had no problem taking his weight. A third plank was laid and another alongside it.

"Well, are ya goin' ta come? Make history?" said Po smiling at Red.

"No, I'll let you history makers go ahead. I'll just wait here."

"Wee girls' knickers," sneered Po.

Again, he got the two finger answer.

Po continued slowly along the first planks and kept going until he was on the second two where he stopped and looked around.

"Safe as houses," laughed Po, who was now about ten feet from the bank.

"Ah, so yis have changed your wee minds after all," smiled Po, as Red and Anto got up and moved toward the edge of the bank. Both knelt down and grabbed a plank each and pulled them out of the glar. This left Po standing on two side by side planks right in the middle. Red and Anto carried the planks a few yards down the bank and threw them into the middle of the glar, out of reach. They did the same with all the other planks still on the bank.

"What the frig are yis doin'?" panted Po.

"Nothin'," said Anto, as he and Red sat down in their original watching position.

"Yis threw ma planks in the glar."

Red turned and looked at Anto.

"He misses nothin'. You'll not get much past our Po."

"You're right. Smart as an auld fox, so he is."

"Smarter, I would say," said Red, seriously.

"I wouldn't disagree with ya there."

"Ah come on lads, quit the messin'. How will a get back ta the bank now?"

"De ya know Po, as well as being smart, sure you're a mind reader. I was just this minute thinkin' the very same thing," said Anto, seriously.

"Ya'll not believe this Anto, but sure wasn't I just thinkin' the very same thing, too?" exclaimed Red.

"Ya were not!" said Anto, looking surprised.

"De ya know, come ta think of it, that makes Po a double mind reader," pointed out Red.

"Come on lads, yis can't leave me standin' here, so ya can't," pleaded Po.

"Is he right, Red? Can we not leave him there?"

"Do ya know, I do believe for once, he's wrong. We can leave him there, not a bother."

"How deep de ya think that glar is, Red?" asked Dunno.

"Wow, let's see. I would say maybe three feet, at least."

"De ya know lads, this is all very interestin' and stuff, but the fact is I'm starvin'. Now if yis would like ta join us, Dunno and Ginger. Free chips for all." Anto got a round of applause.

"Red, Anto, come on now. Seriously, yis can't leave me here. Yous are ma mates."

"Did a tell ya what he did yesterday, with the bucket of slops, and all over your good coat, too?"

"Ya did, Anto. Terrible thing to do on a mate."

"Well sure, ya needn't worry too much, Po. The tide should be in at about three. That's in about an hour and sure you'll be able ta swim out, then."

"No way Anto, he can't do that. Sure, when the water covers the planks they'll only give way, altogether," pointed out Red.

"Never thought a that, Red."

"I was thinkin', he could strip naked, throw his clothes ta the bank and wade across through the glar," advanced Red.

"But sure, how would he get home? He couldn't put his clothes on and he's not goin' ta walk home in his birthday suit."

"This is true Anto, and he would be pure black and stinkin' with his wee black willie just hangin' there."

"This is all great craic, but I'm hungry. We can talk about it at the café," suggested Anto.

All agreed and left, with Po's pleas, threats and swearing ringing in their ears.

As they walked back up the road Anto turned to Red.

"Did ya hear the language of that Po fella? And him an altar boy, too!"

"An absolute and total disgrace."

"That's what it was."

"It was awful, in fact, come ta think of it, his language was just 'glarful'."

All four laughed long and hard.

An hour later, the day's centre of attraction walked into Uncle Luigi's Café seemingly none the worse for the experience.

"Well will ya look who's arrived? Sit your wee self down here, Po, and tell us all the excitin' things ya got up to today," said Anto.

"Well, I have these two whores, fruits, bastards, humpy friggers, who think they are my mates."

"Ah now, that's not nice now Po, ta be talkin' about Dunno and Ginger like that behind their backs. If they were still here they would be cut ta the bone, so they would," said Red.

"Po, I was just wonderin', why are ya glarin' at me?" asked Anto.

Both he and Red burst into loud laughter.

"Ah sure yis are very funny, altogether," mocked Po.

Red placed his hand on his heart.

"It is a glar better thing I do . . ."

"Funny, funny, laugh, laugh," sneered Po.

It turned out that Anto had chatted to some workmen he knew at Newry Town FC, which happened to be quite near to where Po was. He explained the trick they were playing on Po and had arranged with them to get him out in about 15 minutes after they left. They had a ladder and were able to extricate him safely.

The glar jokes lasted almost two days, to Po's annoyance. However, the thoughts of revenge occupied his time, and even the thoughts of it, brought a broad grin to his face.

'I'll get them two buggers if it kills me,' Po promised himself as he turned into Uncle Luigi's Café. He stopped dead just inside the door. The floor had just been washed and there was a cone on the floor with a note stuck to it.

Please be 'glarful', wet floor.

He looked up to see Anto's grinning face behind the counter.

'Death is too good for these bastards. I need somethin' far worse,' thought Po.

End

My Ball Rules

1960

"That is total shit so, it is," said Po, angrily.

"Look, I know the rules Po. Look it up, if ya don't believe me. If the goalkeeper takes more than three steps without releasing the ball, it's an indirect free kick," answered Red.

"Ok, let's say the keeper gets the ball and walks along the goal line; are ya sayin' that the other team gets an indirect free kick six inches from the line? Are ya totally outta your tree?"

"A know it sounds weird, but them's the rules."

"Well, in that case, I'm invokin' the My Ball Rules."

"My Ball Rules, what are ya talkin' about?"

"Ya mean, with all your knowledge of soccer rules, ya've never heard of My Ball Rules?"

"No."

"Too bad. As of now, this match is over and we've won."

"Hi, wait a friggin' minute. Ya can't do that. Sure, there's another fifteen minutes left."

"What's the score?"

"Yous are leadin', 7 ta 6."

"So, we win."

"No, ya don't."

"Yeah, we do."

"Time's not up, yet."

"My Ball Rules."

"What are ya talkin' about?"

"Look, who owns this ball?"

"You do."

"So, meself and my ball are goin' home."

"You're cheatin', so ya are."

"My Ball Rules."

"That's a load a shit. There's no such thing."

"Ok, look at it this way. I am not playin' any more. I'm goin' home, is that ok?"

"That's fine."

"Ok, see ya later."

"Hi, wait a minute. We want ta play on and finish the game, even if you don't."

"Well, I hope ya win. Best a luck."

"But we have no ball."

"Ya noticed?"

"Ya can't take the ball."

"Why?"

"The game's not over."

"But I'm goin' home."

"Well, leave the ball, then."

"And have all you guys kickin' it, that don't know the rules. Don't think so. Get your own ball, mine's comin' home."

"All right. So what de ya want?"

"Want?"

"Want."

"Jasus, sure, I don't want anythin' a'tall."

"Ya want the friggin' rule changed about the goalkeeper, don't ya?"

"Sure, ya can't just go round changin' the rules. Ya said it was in the rules, so ya can't change it then, can ya?" smiled Po.

"If we want ta finish the game we'll have ta change it, won't we?"

"That's a good point."

"So?"

"So what?"

"Are ya goin' ta finish the game?"

"Naw, don't think so. Rules are terrible, so they are."

"Ok, smart arse. So what happens if the keeper walks more than three steps without bouncin' the ball?"

"Oh, I know that rule. Ya get an indirect free kick from outside the box."

"Do ya?"

"Ya do."

"Right, deal. Can we get on with the game now, ya wee whore?"

"Jasus, sure ya can't be doin' that."

"What?"

"Callin' the owner of the ball bad and rude names."

"Oh, sorry. A didn't mean it fartface. Very sorry."

"That's breakin' rule 19 of the My Ball Rules."

"Ok, tell me."

"Rule 19 clearly states, 'Any player who calls the owner of the ball a bad or rude name shall therefore pay the same owner of the ball a sixpence fine'."

"I see, ok. Ya are a wee bastardin', whorein' frigger with a willie that birds mistake for a worm. You're a fruit, with a face so ugly that scares kids. Ya're the worst footballer in the summer league."

"Ah, Jasus, there was no need for that remark about the football, that's way below the belt, so it is. Right, then," Po began counting on his fingers. "I make it that ya owe me a half a crown for insults and name callin'."

"Right. I will owe it to ya. Can we get on now?"

"Sure."

Red pulled the ball from Po and walked off to get the game restarted. Over his shoulder Po heard the word . . .

"Shithead."

"I heard that. That's three bob now!"

End

The Bet

1960

"Will he go for it, do ya think?" asked Red.

"That greedy wee bastard? He'd walk ta Belfast for sixpence," answered Po.

"And ya know he has money?" asked Red.

"I was standin' behind him in the shop, so a was. He must have a pound in his pocket, at least, didn't I tell ya?"

"I told ya he owes me two bob this past month. When I asked him for it, an hour ago, he told me he was broke. Shitfaced, wee, lyin' bastard."

"Shush, here he comes," whispered Po.

"Well boys, what's the craic?" asked Dumpy Loughran, smiling.

"Not much, except for him gettin' on my nerves," said Red.

"What did he do, now?"

"I told him it would be possible ta climb up a rope, without stoppin', ta the top window at the back of my house. But, no, he is too much of a cowardy custard ta take the challenge."

"I'm not a coward, a just think it's too high, that's all," mumbled Po.

"Yeah, right. I bet him four bob it could be done, but no, too high," sneered Red.

"Wait a minute. Ya bet him four bob he couldn't climb up a rope to your top window without stoppin', right?"

"Right."

"Can I take the bet?"

"Ya think ya can climb ta my top window, Dumpy? Ya need to go and see the doctor, so ya do," laughed Red.

"I'll take your bet right now, so a will."

Red looked at Po.

"Is he serious?"

"Seems ta be."

"Ok, Dumpy, ya have a bet. I am bettin' ya four bob ya can't climb to our top window without stoppin'. Deal?"

"Deal. Easiest money I'll make this week," smiled Dumpy shaking hands with Red.

They all went to Red's house and into the back yard. Red got a rope and looked up at the top window.

"Three stories high, Jasus, don't know if even I could do it. Are ya sure ya don't want ta back out now, Dumpy?"

"Are ya crazy? No way," laughed Dumpy.

Red went into the house and climbed the stairs to the top floor. He opened the back window and looked down at Dumpy and Po.

"Right, here comes the rope."

He dropped down one end of the rope, which was caught by Po.

"I have secured this end, it won't slip," shouted Red.

"Ok, Dumpy, off ya go. Put your money where your mouth is," smiled Po. Dumpy began climbing the rope, using his feet against the wall, and pulling himself up, hand over hand. He was, in fact, climbing quite fast. When he was three quarters of the way up he heard Red's voice.

"Hi, Dumpy?" shouted Red. "Did a show ya my new knife?"

"What?" panted Dumpy.

Red held out a 'Jim Bowie' knife with an eight inch long blade.

"This thing's like a razor blade, so it is. Wait till ya see how quick it cuts through this rope."

"Red, Red, what are ya doin'? Don't cut the friggin' rope, for God's sake."

"Now Dumpy, will ya settle down, sure it's only about 50 feet, so it is. Sure I've jumped higher."

"I'll break my legs, Red, if a fall."

"He could get killed, Red, ya know?" shouted up Po.

"I know, I know. Sad havin' ta go ta your grave owin' your friends money, so it is."

"Does he owe money, Red?" shouted Po.

"Sure does. Owes me two bob, so he does."

"Jasus, two bob, is it? That's terrible. Would he not give it back ta ya after ya bein' so good as ta lend it in the first place?"

"Naw, keeps tellin' me he's broke. Anyway Po, watch this knife cut the rope. It'll go through it like butter, so it will."

"I'll give ya the two bob when a get ta the top. Don't cut the rope, Red, please," pleaded Dumpy.

"What did he say, Po? Couldn't hear him right."

"He says, he'll give ya the money he owes ya, when he gets ta the top," shouted Po.

"Is that what ya said, Dumpy?" asked Red.

"Right. That's what a said. I'll give ya the two bob when a get to the top. Will ya hurry up, Red, ma arms are gettin' tired here."

"Ok, well let's see now. Ya borrowed two bob. That was some time ago, now. So, with interest, since you're my friend and all that, another two bob interest, and sure we will call it quits."

"That's four bob?"

"Jasus, did ya hear that, he can count well, so he can."

Red placed the knife on the rope.

"Ok, ok. Four bob."

"Sure will ya just drop it down ta Po, there. Not that a wouldn't trust ya, or anything."

Dumpy, with much moaning and groaning, managed to get a hand into his pocket and extracted some money. He dropped one two shilling piece and two single shillings to Po.

Red began lowering the rope and Dumpy eventually reached the ground, looking quite flushed. He left without even saying goodbye. Red arrived at Po's side and they went down the back and perched themselves on a wall. Red gave Po a shilling for his trouble, kissed the three shillings, and put them in his pocket.

"Now was that an interestin' episode?" smiled Po.

"It was, it was. I'm beginnin' ta like this business stuff," laughed Red.

End

The Message Boy

1960

Red Morgan walked around the packed storeroom of Peter Regan's Grocery Shop on Newry's Mill Street. This was the first day of his summer job as a Message Boy and he was getting to know, as instructed by his new boss, the layout of the store. He was told to familiarise himself as to where the goods were stored, as from that day, he would be filling the orders that were to be delivered to the customers.

Red loved the smells that the store produced. The odours came from an array of disinfectants, soaps, household cleaning products, to washing powders and even chests of tea.

"Red?" came the voice of Mary Dooley, one of the ladies that worked in the shop.

"Yes," answered Red, as he hurried along the yard between the shop and the store to meet her.

"Got a run for you. Will ya fill this list from the store and I will do the meats and cheese from the shop."

"Sure, right away," said Red, taking the list from Mary.

"It's for one of our regular customers, Mrs. Cummings. She lives at the top of Daisy Hill."

Red filled a cardboard box with the required items from the store and proceeded to the shop.

"Now Red, will ya look outside, it is bucketin' down, so ya'll need your rainwear. It's hangin' in the back hall."

Red proceeded to the back hall and took down a pair of black oilskin trousers and a large matching cape and southwester hat. He donned the rainwear and returned to the shop.

Mary had placed a smaller box inside the box Red filled from the store, with bacon, sausages, eggs and butter. She then covered the box with a large plastic bag to keep the rain out.

"There's her receipt, Red. Make sure ya keep it dry. Now she lives at the very top of the hill. It's the last house on the left, ok?"

"No problem, I'll find it ok," smiled Red.

He carried the cardboard box outside to his black messenger bicycle, which was parked on the footpath. The front of the bike had a large, square, metal box holder. A wooden box had already been placed in it. Red placed the grocery box inside it and began his first delivery.

There were no gears on the message bike and it was quite heavy, with the extra weight of the metal box holder in the front, plus a piece of sheet metal covering the middle of the bike advertising 'Regan's Groceries'. The rain was very heavy as Red made his way across Lower Mill Street, then Francis Street, until he reached the Pound Road where he stopped and looked up at the steep Daisy Hill in front of him. There was no way he could ride the heavy bike up that hill. It was now a matter of pushing it, all the way to the top.

It was still raining heavily as Red began the, almost, one-mile climb up Daisy Hill. He had to stop a number of times on the way, to rest, but finally got there in under twenty minutes. The house was easy to find and he knocked on the door. A small, stout, grey-haired lady opened the door. "Yes?"

"Delivery from Regan's, missus," said Red.

"Oh, right, just sit it here, on the mat. I don't want you drippin' all over my floor."

Red did as he was told and as he looked up to say goodbye. He just managed to get his face out of the way of the slamming door. 'What an old bag' he thought.

Going back was easy, all downhill. He made it back to the shop in under ten minutes. As he walked in, Mary called him. She had a broad grin on her face.

"Red, ya will just love this."

"What?" smiled Red.

"Mrs. Cummings just rang. She forgot to order bread and wants it, right away."

"You're jokin', right?"

"Fraid not. Here," said Mary, handing Red a McCann's Bakery loaf.

Red just took the loaf and nodded. He got back on his bike and retraced his journey to Mrs. Cummings' hilltop residence.

'This job was a big mistake. If it is goin' ta be like this, I'm packin' it in this week' thought Red.

He knocked the door which was opened immediately by Mrs. Cummings. She took the bread from Red's hands.

"Oh for God's sake, I wanted a sliced loaf, this is a plain one. I suppose it'll have ta do."

The door slammed again. Red stood for a moment looking at the door, rain running down his face.

"That's ok, Mrs. Cummings, no need for thanks, sure it was a pleasure. You have a nice day too," he mumbled.

*   *   *

Red was sitting in Uncle Luigi's with Po and Anto.

"If it had a been me a would have told her ta get stuffed," said Anto seriously.

"Believe me, I felt like it," replied Red.

"Friggin' auld bitch," added Po.

"Well Po, you're the planner, aren't ya? So, come up with somethin' to get this auld bitch," smiled Red.

"Sure it'll be a total pleasure, so it will," laughed Po.

A few days later Po called to Red's house and found him weeding the garden at the back.

"That auld bat ya were tellin' us about, what's the sides of her house like?" asked Po.

"The sides? Ya mean the ground?"

"Yeah."

"There's just the path up ta the door. The sides of the house are just clay and get muddy when it rains, why?"

"I have an idea ta teach the auld frigger a lesson."

"Tell me."

"Well the idea is ta jam her front door the night before ya know ya are deliverin', but it has ta be rainin', that's important. When is she due a delivery?"

"First thing in the mornin'."

"Brilliant, it's rainin' now, so the ground will be well muddy."

"Ya've lost me altogether. What are ya plannin'?"

"We are goin' up there tonight. I'll tell ya all then. Meet ya here at eleven, right?"

"Ok, suppose so," smiled Red.

Red and Po arrived at Mrs. Cummings' house just before midnight.

"Jasus, ya have ta push a message bike up this friggin' hill?"

"Yep."

"Rather you than me," panted Po.

"So what are we for doin', then?"

Po began fumbling with his coat pocket and produced a small wedge of wood. He showed it to Red.

"Now, this is the baby that will do the damage," whispered Po.

"What?"

"Now, we need ta get ta the front door, nice and quiet. Come on . . ."

Next morning it was still raining as Red arrived, out of breath, at Mrs. Cummings' house. He rapped the door and waited. There was some fumbling and grumbling from the other side of the door.

"Who is it?" shouted Mrs. Cummings through the letterbox.

"Delivery from Ragan's, missus."

"My door is jammed. Ya'll have ta bring it around the back," replied Mrs. Cummings.

"Can't do that missus," Red replied.

"What do ya mean, ya can't do that?" snarled Mrs. Cummings.

"Well, ya remember the first day I delivered your groceries? It was rainin' heavy and ya didn't want me to get your lovely hall wet?"

"So what?"

"Well, ya see, the side of your house is all muddy and I am not goin' ta get my new shoes wet and muddy. I have ta work in them all day."

"Oh, for God's sake. Stay there an' I'll come round and get them."

Red heard the back door open. A few minutes later he heard mumbling and swearing.

Mrs. Cummings appeared around the corner.

"Would ya look at the state of ma shoes and feet, would ya?" snarled Mrs. Cummings.

"Terrible, so it is, missus, just terrible. They look all wet and covered in mud."

Mrs. Cummings muttered something inaudible, took the box of groceries from Red and, without another word, headed back around the corner to the rear of the house. When she had turned the corner, Red produced a screwdriver from his pocket, bent down and pried loose the wedge of wood jammed under the door. As Red reached the gate, he heard a shout from the side of the house, followed by some more loud mutterings. He free wheeled his bike down the road a little, to where he could see the side of the house where he observed a quite irate Mrs. Cummings picking up groceries that had spilled out into the mud from the box she had just dropped. Red took off down the hill with a broad grin across his face.

"Did it work?" asked Po, as Red sat down in the first snug beside Po, in Uncle Luigi's.

"Worked a friggin' treat. She even dropped the box in the mud at the side of the house," laughed Red.

"Bloody great! Couldn't have been better," roared Po.

Red's coffee arrived with Anto who, of course, wanted to hear every detail.

Po lifted his coffee and clinked Red's cup.

"Here's hopin' the auld bitch has learned a lesson. Never be nasty ta message boys, brings nothin' but mud and wet feet."

End

Hello Dublin

1960

It was the last week in school ever, for the class of 3C. Now their school days were coming to an end and all would be leaving to face the big, wide world. Poor world! There were stories that the teachers even held a party to celebrate 3C's departure. No more anti-depressants, no more worries, no more nervous tension. From here on they would be dealing with normal, everyday students who would not shorten their lives.

Some of the boys in 3C already had jobs lined up with fathers, uncles or family friends, to start careers in Carpentry, Brick Laying, Plumbing, and, in one case, a trainee Mortician. Those that were left, including Red, Dunno, Po, Jumpy, Ginger and Bishop were told to report to the Assembly Hall after school that Wednesday, at three fifteen. When they arrived they were all lined up and introduced to a well-dressed, small, stout, tanned, balding man named Mr. Dupree. He ran a clothing manufacturing business in Dublin. It was their intention to open a factory in Newry within the next few months and they needed trainees from the area to get the factory up and running. These trainees would be taken to their Dublin business, to learn the job for a period of three months.

Mr. Dupree spoke to all the boys individually, and selected twenty of the forty assembled, which included Red, Jumpy, and Po. The Bishop, Ginger and Dunno were also chosen. They were told they would all be receiving letters of confirmation in the post within the next few days, detailing arrangements for travel, etc.

The following Monday, Red received his letter from Mr. Dupree, which informed him he was to be at Edward Street Railway Station on the coming Friday morning, at ten fifteen, for the trip to Dublin.

"Well, now that all the ballyhoo is over, how do ya feel about headin' off to the big city, on Friday?" asked Anto, sitting across from Red and Po in Uncle Luigi's Café.
"Lookin' forward to it. Dublin's a fantastic city," answered Red.
"Me too," added Po, excitedly.
"We might not even like it, ya know. At the end of the day, we will just have to wait and see," said Red.
"I think yis are lucky bastards. Big city, loads to do, loads of beautiful women, wow!"
"There's that, but I will miss ya so much, Anto, I might cry an' come home," said Red, placing his hand gently on Anto's face.
"Piss off, ya queer," snarled Anto. "There'll be plenty a fruits in Dublin for ya. Shirt-lifters by the dozen."
They all laughed and got back to their Cokes.

The few days before the great departure passed quite quickly for Red and Po. They had to be bought new toothbrushes, pyjamas, face cloths, towels, and in Po's case, his mom even packed toilet paper! So, Friday morning arrived and they were all standing with their bulging suitcases on the platform of Edward Street Railway Station. It was a dark place, with a strong smell of steam, oil and coal in the air. There was much excitement as the boys greeted each other, on arrival. Most of the parents had come along to see their little angels off on their great adventure. They obviously had scant knowledge of their own kids, angels? That might be stretching it a tad!

Eventually, they boarded the Dublin train and some five minutes later, with a jolt, they were on their way. There was great cheering and much waving, with damp handkerchiefs in abundance. Goodbyes being shouted, followed by, "be good boys, behave yourselves, good luck, write soon, send a postcard."

The train left the station and a silence dropped around them all. They were, at last, on their way. Everyone was deep in their own thoughts. No more bossy sisters, no more young brothers, no more moms or dads, no more messages or chores, no more school. They were free!

An hour and a half later they arrived in Dublin's Amiens Street Station, and were met by some of the company's staff. There were a number of photographers and reporters there to greet them, also. This, no doubt, was organised by the company. The publicity machine was in full swing.

Eventually they were all dropped off in groups at Guest Houses and Bed and Breakfasts in the Drumcondra and Glasnevin areas of the city with the orders that they were to get settled in. The company minibus would be picking them up in an hour when they were to be given a tour of the factory.

Red, Po, Jumpy, Dunno and The Bishop all made sure they were in the same digs. Red and Po had a room to themselves. The Bishop and the other two shared another room. The house was modern and comfortable with a large TV lounge on the second floor. There was even a maid, who they all thought was a 'doll', even though she had a weird accent.

An hour later, on time, the minibus arrived and took them to the factory, which was less than a mile away, opposite a large park, where Red made particular note of lots of well-tended football pitches. Inside, the factory was a huge place. The main area was divided into two sections. On the left there were dozens of sewing machines set twelve to a bench, six on each side. On the other side of the huge floor were long work tables where, the boys were told, most of them would be working. They were given a tour of all the work areas, the cutting room, canteen, toilets, storerooms and offices.

"Jasus, this is some place," commented Bishop Keenan.
"That it is," answered Po, looking around the enormous factory.
"And would ya look at the women. Jasus, they're gorgeous, so they are."
"De ya think I haven't noticed?" smiled Red.

One girl, in particular, caught Red's eye. She had short, blond hair with big, blue eyes. When she caught him looking at her she smiled and blushed. Red felt his heart jump.

Red and Po were assigned to a bench on the right-hand side of the factory floor. They were told they would be known as 'Makers'. It would be their job to stick and tape the coats together, before they were sewn.

*   *   *

"Well, are we goin' into the city, then?" asked Po, coming into the bedroom.
It was now after six in the evening, and everyone was continuing to get settled in and unpacked. Red looked up at Po. He was reading a Dublin newspaper, which he had found on the living room coffee table.
"Sounds like an idea ta me. Who all's goin'?" he asked.
"I think everyone is, leavin' in five minutes," answered Po.
"Ok, meet ya downstairs."

They caught the city centre bus on the Glasnevin Road, which took ten minutes to reach O'Connell Street, in the centre of Dublin.
"Where will we go?" asked Bishop Keenan.
"Does anyone fancy goin' ta the pictures? I saw an ad in the paper for a cinema called the Royal. They have a cabaret on stage before the movie, and the movie is in 3D. I have always wanted ta see one of them films," said Red.
"What's a cabaret?" asked Jumpy.
"Like a concert, with dancers, music, comics and all that," answered Red.
"Wow, sounds great. And will there be girl dancers?"
"No, just old men in their sixties, twit," laughed Red.
"Red, what is 3D?" asked Dunno.
"Sorta hard to explain. Ya have ta wear these coloured glasses they give ya, and they make things look like they are comin' outta the screen."
"Wow! I want ta see that," said Jumpy.

It was agreed by all to go to the Royal Cinema. They got the cheapest tickets they could, which were on the second balcony, high into the roof of the great theatre. They were given their cardboard 3D glasses, which had coloured plastic lenses.

The Theatre Royal, was a large art deco building, designed for an audience of three thousand seven hundred people seated and three hundred, standing. It was intended for use as both Cinema and Theatre. It also housed the Regal Rooms Restaurant. The theatre had a resident twenty five piece orchestra and a troupe of dancers called the Royalettes.

The boys were amazed at the size of the place, and were discussing it when the music started and the lighting went down. The great golden curtains began to open, showing a large stage filled with dancing girls. The lads were all in a state of awe, both at the dancing girls, and the size and grandeur of the theatre. The show, that night, had comics, singers, dancers, Irish music, and a magician. It was enjoyed by all. The boys applauded loudly, and cheered after every single act.

It was now the intermission and the lights came up and the curtains closed. Girls, with square wooden trays strapped around their necks, selling ice cream, crisps and sweets walked down all the aisles and took up positions at the front of the balcony. Some of the boys joined the queue and bought ice cream and sweets. Some ten minutes later, the lights went down and the curtains opened to expose an enormous screen, which immediately burst into life. There were some advertisements for up-coming films and stage events. Then the theatre went dark. A notice on the screen advised the watching audience to don their 3D glasses. The movie '13 Ghosts' began.

After just a few minutes into the movie, the audience were gasping as the screen characters seemed to be coming towards them. The movie got quite scary at times and Red noticed a few of his friends had looked away from the screen, or were sitting with their mouths open.
"Have ya any matches?" Red whispered to Po.
"No. Jumpy has them," he whispered back.
Jumpy was sitting on the other side of Po. He reached behind Po, and tapped Jumpy on the shoulder. Jumpy screamed, and jumped out of his seat, totally forgetting his carton of Coke which drenched himself and, both, Po and Dunno.
"Jasus, Jumpy, what the shit are ya doin'?" complained Po, wiping himself down.

"Somethin' touched me," answered Jumpy, in a shaky voice.

After the movie they crossed O'Connell Bridge into O'Connell Street, to get their bus back home. The street was brightly lit with many neon signs and displaying ads for Cafés, Cinemas, Businesses and Shops. It was packed with thousands of people, from many nationalities. The boys were wide-eyed at the sights and sounds of the city.

"Jasus, this is some place," commented Po.

"That it is, for sure. Outside of a football match, I've never seen so many people," said Bishop.

"Did ya see that, did ya?" said an excited Jumpy, looking behind.

"See what?" asked Red.

"Them two birds that passed smiled at me."

"Jumpy, anyone that's never seen ya before smiles when they see ya for the first time," laughed Red.

"Very funny," sulked Jumpy.

They got their bus and made it home safe and sound, chatting all the time about the movie, the theatre, the acts and Dublin, in general. Their first day in Dublin was at an end. A great adventure was to follow, with every day bringing something new and exciting into their lives.

End

First Day at Work

1960

Everyone arrived early for their first day at work and all were assigned their jobs. Red and Po were placed at a long work bench, which they would share with eight others. There was an experienced worker on each bench to teach the boys their jobs. Willie Roach was their instructor.

They were each given a tin mug filled with a grey glue. They were shown what to do with it, using their index finger to scoop out some of the glue and work it onto the top of their index finger, using the lip of the mug. On a rail behind them they had the 'facings' of waterproof coats. Their job was to smear the glue, about one inch wide, along the edges of the facing. They came in batches of 20. When they were all done, they would go back to the beginning and take the first one they had smeared. By this time, the glue had dried. The edge was folded over on itself, all the way around. Then, a small metal wheel, about two inches wide, with a wooden handle was used to roll the edges, flattening them out to make the glue stick tight. Then another tool, a metal wheel with dry glue wrapped around it was used. This was pressed along the edge of the fold, to remove all excess glue. When these were all done they were transferred to the machinists. The same techniques were used on the backs, lapels and collars of the coats. The machinists would sew them together. When this process was completed, the coats were returned to the benches and the seams were glued again, this time with tape laid over them, totally covering the joint. The wheel was then used to remove excess glue, thus making all the seams completely waterproof.

At lunchtime they all met up in the large factory canteen for dinner.

"Not the easiest job I've ever done," said Red, to all at the table.

"Goin' ta take awhile ta get the hang of usin' the glue, for sure," said Bishop.

"Can get messy, too," added Po.

"Yeah, I noticed that. Ya had more glue on your apron than on the coat," laughed Bishop.

"You're such a wise arse Keenan. Ya weren't too great with it, your own self," snapped Po.

"Now Po, behave your wee self. We don't want any sticky moments here, now do we?" said Red slowly, pointing his finger at Po.

This got a round of applause from all at the table, even Po.

"Nice one, Red. You keep it up and one of these days ya'll get that second brain cell workin'," smiled Po. This caused more laughter from the gathering.

"I'm heading over ta the park for a while, anyone comin'?" said Red.

There were a few 'yeas' and they left the factory, crossed the road into the park. They occupied the first seat they reached, facing the river.

"Jasus, a could sleep, so a could," said Jumpy, lying down on the grass.

"Is your poor, wee self tired, Jumpy?" smiled Po.

"I couldn't get ta sleep last night, so a couldn't."

"Were ya havin' sexy dreams, were ya?" continued Po.

"No, nightmares he was havin'. He was dreamin' about you," laughed Bishop.

The boys chatted for another fifteen minutes, at which time Po looked at his watch.

"Jasus, it's five ta two. We'd better get goin'."

"What about sleepin' beauty there?" asked Bishop.

"Ah, the poor, wee man needs his sleep. Let's just leave him," smiled Po. Everyone giggled and quietly left.

"Red, look who's turned up," smiled Po.

Red looked up and spotted Jumpy walking towards them. Then he looked at his watch. It was almost 3pm.

"Yis are a bunch of bastards, and shits, and whores and fruits," snarled Jumpy, as he arrived at the bench.

"Red, who is Jumpy talkin' about?"

"No idea. Couldn't be us. Must be these other lads at the next table."

"Yis left me there sleepin', so yis did."

"Were ya sleepin', Jumpy? Jasus, sure a never noticed," said Po, seriously.

"Jumpy, what happened ta your neck?"

Red noticed the left side of Jumpy's neck was swollen and red.

"I got stung by a bee or a wasp or somethin', so a did. Friggin' sore, too."

"Ah, ya poor, wee soldier. Ya better go ta the First Aid and get it looked at," said Red.

"I'm not goin' ta any First Aid friggin' room."

"Ya hear that Po? He's not goin'. Wish it was me, I can tell ya. Did ya see the size of that nurse's yokes, did ya? Jasus, I wouldn't mind her bendin' over me," said Red, seriously.

"Well Jumpy, up ta your own self . . . Hi, where did he go?"

Red looked around just in time to see Jumpy disappearing through the door of the First Aid room.

"Did ya see this, Red?" asked Po, as he set down the bundle he had just collected from the 'Cutters' room.

"What is it?"

"It's called snap wire."

"What's it for?"

"They tie up scraps with it in the Cutters room, so they do."

"An' what do ya want with it?"

"Haven't decided, just yet. Ya see that clip, when ya snap it closed it can't be opened again. Has ta be cut, so it does," smiled Po.

"No doubt, knowin' you, ya'll find some devious use for it. It had just better not have anythin' ta do with me. Consider yourself well warned."

Po looked up at the clock. It was close to 5.30pm.

"Red, we're finishin' in a few minutes, so we are. Who do I owe a favour ta, here at the bench?"

Red looked around.

"Well, Ginger, over there, stole your tie last night."

"That's it, Ginger bastard."

Po looked around to make sure no one was watching. He crept along his side of the bench, out of sight of the lads on the other side. Ginger was working at the very end of the bench. Po crept on hands and knees under the table and in seconds wrapped the wire around Ginger's leg and the bench leg, snapping the clasp closed.

"What the shit?" Ginger looked under the table, to see Po waving.

"What did ya friggin' do, ya wee bastard?"

Ginger's leg was fixed firmly to the bench. Just then the horn went off, which indicated the end of the working day and everyone began to leave the factory.

"Po, get me outta this, ya wee frigger!"

"I'll teach ya not ta be stealin' ma ties, so a will."

Red and Po were on their way home when the Bishop caught up with them.

"Ya got Ginger well, Po. How will he get free?"

"Someone will get the cutters and cut the wire," smiled Po.

"Yeah, suppose. Poor Ginger," laughed Bishop.

So ended workday one, an eventful, interesting and learning day for the boys.

End

Red's Big Date

1960

Red and Po were sitting in the factory canteen, on their tea break.
"Why don't ya just go up ta her and ask her out, ya coward?" asked Po.
"Because," mumbled Red.
"Because what?"
"Just because. Will ya get off my friggin' back, ya nag?"
"Look, she's just sittin' over there. Go and ask her out, for Christ's sake."
"No."
"I thought ya fancied her?"
"I do."
"So?"
"Time's not right."
"Time's not right," mocked Po. "That's crap, and ya know it."
Just then Red's dream woman, who they had been introduced to some days earlier, called Marian, rose and left her table.
"Ya missed your chance again, ya plank," sneered Po.
"I'll ask her tomorrow."
"Yeah, course ya will. I'm goin' for a leak."

Po got up and left quickly. He caught up with Marian in the corridor.
"Marian, hold up a minute."

"Hi, Po," smiled Marian.

"I have somethin' ta ask ya."

"Ask away."

"Do ya fancy Red a'tall?"

"What?"

"Do ya fancy him?"

"He's nice, why?"

"He wants ta ask ya out, but hasn't got the nerve."

Marian laughed.

"Really, hmm, I see. Leave it with me, then," she smiled.

Po returned to the canteen and joined Red again.

"So are ya goin' ta ask her out tomorrow then, for sure?"

"Didn't I say a would, didn't I?"

"Believe it when I see it."

Red looked up and saw Marian approaching his table. He swallowed.

"Hi, Red," she smiled.

"Hello, Marian," he managed to get out.

"Are ya doin' anythin' tonight?"

"No, no, nothin', no."

"Will ya take me to the pictures?"

"The pictures?"

Po's shoe made hard contact with Red's shin.

"Yes, I'd love ta, Marian. Love ta."

"Great. Meet me at Clerys on O'Connell Street at eight o'clock, ok?"

"Ok, I'll see ya there."

Marian smiled and left. Red watched her all the way to the door. She was tall with short blond hair, very large blue eyes and, according to Red, the best legs he had ever seen.

"Well, what de ya think of that, lucky bastard?" grinned Po.

"I think a just died and went ta heaven."

*   *   *

That evening, after dinner, there was a combined effort to get Red out the door in a presentable fashion. He was ordered to the bathroom and told to scrub every inch. During this time, Po was ironing his trousers and shirt,

Bishop was selecting a tie and Ginger was polishing his shoes. When he was dressed and brushed down, they all stood back and examined their work.

"What de ya think?" asked Bishop.

"So, so. Pity about the face, isn't it. Can we not do anythin' with it, de ya think?" asked Ginger, rubbing his chin.

"Is there a hammer in the house?" asked Po.

"I'll go and look," said Bishop.

"No messin'. Do a look all right?" asked Red, seriously.

"Well, all right ya ask? I would say ya would pass with a shove, just," smiled Po.

"Will ya get your arse in gear, will ya? The friggin' clock's tickin'," said Ginger.

Red left the house and walked to Drumcondra Road, where he got a bus to the city centre. He arrived at Clerys shop half an hour early, according to the large clock hanging over the door. At ten past eight, he had just finished his fifth Woodbine when he spotted Marian walking towards him. To say she looked beautiful would have been an understatement. She was dressed in a short blue mini dress that showed off her shapely legs. It had a jacket to match. He found it hard to breathe, and was lucky to even get 'hello' out. They decided to go to the Savoy Cinema on O'Connell Street and see a horror movie called 'The Fall of the House of Usher' with Vincent Price and Mark Damon.

*   *   *

Just before midnight Red walked into the TV lounge to find everyone waiting up for him. The coffee table was littered with cold chips and bread. He was ushered into an armchair in the corner. The TV was turned off.

"Tell everything," said Po.

"Leave nothing out, either," added Bishop.

"Details, details," put in Ginger.

"Well, let's see. When I saw her tonight for the first time, all dressed up with the make-up and everything, Jasus, she was beautiful. I thought she was a good lookin' girl at work, when I looked at her tonight, sure a nearly fainted. Give us a drink of that Coke."

"Will ya get on with it, will ya?" prompted Po, giving him the Coke.

"She was beautiful, no, spectacular. She looked like a movie star, so she did. I just wanted ta stand on O'Connell Street all night so people would see she was with me."

"Jasus," said Po.

"Holy Jasus," added Ginger.

"Where did yis go?" asked Bishop.

"Went ta the Savoy. There was a horror movie on. Best choice a ever made," laughed Red.

"Why was that?" asked Po, excitedly.

"I was thinkin' ta meself about puttin' my arm around her and how I should go about it. Well, sure when the movie started, every scary thing that came on, she only grabbed me and buried her head in my chest," laughed Red.

"Where did yis go afterwards?" asked Ginger.

"Ya know that wee café next to the Savoy with the good fish and chips? Went in there and had coffee and buns."

"So, did you kiss her before she got on the bus?" asked Po, smiling.

"Got on the bus? Are ya out of your wee mind. De ya think I was goin' to let a walkin' vision like that get on the bus on her own? No way. I went with her to her house in Finglas, so a did."

"He's only right, ya know. Lot of hooligans on the late buses, so there is," put in Bishop, seriously.

"And did ya get a wee kiss and all at the door, did ya?" smiled Po.

"She took me into the house and made me tea."

"Jasus, he got the feet under the friggin' table, so he did," commented Ginger.

"That was the sad part of the night, so it was," went on Red.

"Sad? What de ya mean?" asked Bishop.

"Ya know, havin' ta get outta bed ta come home."

Red was battered with newspapers, cold chips, crusts of bread and was called a few names he had never heard before. When they all left the room, Red looked up smiling.

"Jasus Christ, isn't it a holy terror the way friends behave. No manners. None a'tall."

End

Newry V Dublin

1960

A football match was arranged between the Dublin and Newry workers in the park, facing the factory, on Dublin's Botanic Avenue. Kick off was scheduled for lunchtime on Friday. It was agreed there was to be twenty minutes each half. It took some time to select a neutral referee, but Bob, the foreman from the Cutting Room, was eventually accepted.

"That wee guy, John, is brilliant, so he is. I was playing with him during the week," commented Dunno McManus.

"Dunno, I didn't know ya were like that. Ya dirty wee rat, ya kept that a secret. Did any of you guys know Dunno was a fruit?" said Red, seriously.

"News ta me, but I always knew there was somethin' odd about the way he walked," replied Po.

"Did you notice that, too? I thought it was my imagination. He sort of wiggles like a girl, doesn't he?" added Bishop Keenan.

"Come ta think of it, you're right, Bishop, he does have a wiggle, Dunno, gis a kiss," said Ginger McVerry, grabbing Dunno in a passionate embrace.

"Get off, ya friggin' queer, McVerry. Will yis stop it, will yis. Ya know what I meant. I was playing football with him, so I was," put in Dunno, defensively.

"Yeah. We know, Dunno, we know. Of course ya were," said Red, winking knowingly at Po.

"Don't worry, Dunno. We won't tell anyone, will we Red?" smiled Po.

"Not a one. Never. No way. It will be a secret between us and the people of Newry. We will not tell another soul," laughed Red.

"Bastards," grunted Dunno.

"I was just thinkin' that if Anto were here, there would be a 'book' on the match, and he would have some sort of angle, for sure," laughed Red.

"That he would. He wouldn't miss an opportunity like this," agreed Po.

The boys were on their way to the football pitch. They had decided on the 'top pitch', as it was known, which was high up in the park. A few feet from the sideline there was a steep slope down to the Tolka River that ran through the park.

The referee blew his whistle and the game was on. Within the first five minutes the Newry team scored a goal, and it was Jumpy Jones who did the honours. There was great celebration which lasted until the Dublin team complained they wanted to get on with the game. Just before half-time, the Dublin team scored. The match remained a draw until near the end, when the ball went out of play and Jumpy ran to retrieve it. The ball ran down the slope and Jumpy went after it. Unfortunately, due to the steepness of the slope and the speed with which Jumpy set off, gravity had taken control of the situation and he could not stop running.

"He can't stop," said Po, standing beside Red.

"He's goin' ta end up in the river, wait an' see," replied Red.

Jumpy was screaming as he crossed the path at the bottom of the grassy slope, and made a great splash as he belly flopped into the park river. Luckily, the river was only a few feet deep and in a few moments he stood up, totally soaked, to the somewhat less than sympathetic cheers and applause of both teams. Jumpy stood looking down at himself, holding his arms out as if surprised he was wet. Everyone ran down the slope to where Jumpy was, but with a lot more care than he had done. By the time they got to the river, he had extradited himself and was standing on the pathway.

"Jasus Jumpy, sure that was some dive into the water, so it was," laughed Po.

"It was nothing less than spectacular," added Red.

"Were ya too hot, or what?" asked Bishop.

"He just wanted ta show off his divin' technique, so he did," added Po.

"Frig me, I'm soaked through. What'll a do?" panted Jumpy.

"Well, ta get yourself dry might be a good idea," said Red, seriously.

"How the hell will a do that?" complained Jumpy.

"Let's get back ta the factory and see what we can do," suggested Po.

It was decided to end the match at this time and a draw was agreed by all to be a good result.

Back at the factory, an overcoat was borrowed for Jumpy and his clothes were given to Mrs. Jones, in the canteen, who agreed to dry them for him. Word of Jumpy's adventure had spread throughout the factory, and his arrival on the factory floor, in his newly-acquired overcoat, was waited on by all the girls with great anticipation. When he appeared from the canteen a great cheer went up from all the factory workers, and Jumpy's face got redder by the second. Even the factory foreman covered his mouth to hide a smile. Some of the girls approached Jumpy, trying to pull up the back of his coat, which embarrassed him even more. One in particular, Margaret, was the leader of any and all devilment that went on in the factory. She had one of the machinists approach Jumpy and ask a question about a coat he had finished. While the girl engaged Jumpy in conversation, she managed to get behind Jumpy without being noticed. She got down on her knees and looked up his overcoat. The girl talking to Jumpy looked down at Margaret, the Peeping Tom.

"Well?"

"It was so small I couldn't see it, but he has a nice bum."

All at the bench who were watching what was going on burst into a spontaneous round of loud applause and cheering. Jumpy looked around, then down at Margaret and realised what was going on. His face turned a bright scarlet, to the delight of all watching.

Both teams agreed to hold the Newry V Dublin match every Friday, and from then on it would be called 'The International Splash Football Tournament'. Jumpy would never be allowed to forget his untimely swim in the river. And, of course, the fact that Margaret swore his manliness was so small that she could not see it, did not, in any way, help matters for Jumpy.

End

The Ghost That Was Scared

1960

"So, we'll scare the shit out of them," laughed Jumpy.
"Sounds like a plan, if they go for it," smiled Po.
"They will for sure, we have it all set up," added Dunno.
"Lookin' forward to hear how it turns out. See ya later," smiled Po.

Po dragged Red into the empty TV lounge when they got home from work.
"Let me tell ya what Jumpy and Dunno are up ta."
"Can't wait."
"They plan ta fill the boy's heads with stories about ghosts in Glasnevin Cemetery and take them there tonight."
"Why?"
"Well, Dunno plans to already be there with a mask and a torch. When the boys arrive he will jump up and scare the livin' daylights outta them."
"Very excitin'. Is this what is so secret?"
"Ah, but I have a wee plan."
"I somehow or other thought ya might."

Glasnevin Cemetery is an enormous place situated on the north side of Dublin city. It is said there are more people buried there than now live in Dublin. Many of Ireland's historical figures have been laid to rest there.

"Are ya ready?" asked Po.

"We goin' now?" replied Red.

"Yeah. A wanna be there well before them. Come on, will ya?" said Po, as he dragged Red, by the coat, out of the room.

The two walked the two-mile journey to Glasnevin Cemetery. Making sure there was no one around, they clambered over the railings.

"Where do we go from here?" whispered Red.

"We need ta get as close as we can ta Michael Collins' grave. That's where Jumpy will be takin' the lads. The story he is tellin' them is about Michael Collins' ghost appearin' there, all the time."

"And what happens if it does?"

"Does what?"

"Appear."

"Would ya ever grow up?"

"Well, all the old stories start somewhere and most of them have a grain of truth, ya know?"

"Will ya keep your mind on the job here, ya big ninny."

"An' what about Dunno, where will he be?"

"This, I'm not sure of. We will have to watch for him comin', and get as near as we can without being seen."

Fifteen minutes passed before they heard a noise.

"Did ya hear that?" whispered Po.

"Yeah, de ya think it's Dunno?"

"Would bet on it. He's like a bull in a friggin' china shop."

They caught sight of a shadowy figure moving toward them, stopping every few feet to look around. It was Dunno, all right. He stopped about ten feet from them and crouched down, behind a tall gravestone. Red touched Po's shoulder which made him jump. Red had to use both hands to stifle his giggling.

"Will ya stop friggin' messin', ya whore," Po whispered.

This just made Red worse. Suddenly there was more noise, a lot louder this time. Po elbowed Red and pointed. There were three dark figures slowly moving toward them.

"It's them. Get ready," whispered Po.

The three figures, who Red and Po had identified as, Jumpy, Ginger and Bishop stopped at the grave of Michael Collins, about twenty feet away. There was a lot of whispering between them. Suddenly, Dunno stood up and put the flashlight under his chin, lighting up the monster mask he was wearing. He howled loudly. The three guys stood open-mouthed, staring like deer in the headlights and began to slowly back away.

Po got onto Red's shoulders and pulled the sheet he had borrowed from the linen cupboard over his head. Red lit his flashlight and stood up. Po made a deep growling sound, which he was very good at. The three boys looked, the ghost in the mask looked, and all, as if in a flash, disappeared screaming towards the fence.

Later at the digs, Red and Po walked into the TV lounge.

"Hi boys, yis been out?" asked Po.

"Jasus, ya wouldn't believe it Po, ya just wouldn't," said Ginger.

"Believe what?" asked Red.

"You tell them, Dunno."

"Well, we were goin' ta play a wee trick on the boys, Bishop an' Ginger, here."

"Yeah, ya were tellin' me earlier," said Po, sitting down.

"I went on ahead of them to the graveyard, so a did, and hid, waitin' on them. I was goin' to jump out with ma mask and scare the shit outta them."

"That was great, did they freak out, then?" laughed Red.

"Freak out? Freak out! Nearly friggin' dropped dead on the spot, so a did," panted Dunno, his face losing colour as he remembered.

"What do ya mean?" asked Po, innocently.

"Well, I jumped up, as planned, when they arrived, so a did. I scared the life outta them."

"He did, for sure. Nearly pissed meself, so a did," said Jumpy.

"Well, ya'll not believe what happened next," went on Dunno.

"They fainted?" laughed Po.

"Wait till ya hear this. Just behind me a heard a noise and turned around. I could not believe what I saw."

"What?" asked Red, being very serious.

"There was a shrouded figure rising slowly out of a friggin' grave, so there was."

"Would ya ever get a grip, Dunno. De ya think I'm gonna fall for that?"

"Ask them, I swear on all that's holy, it happened."

"Wait a minute, are ya tellin' us that while you were scarin' the boys here, a real ghost arose behind ya and scared the whole lot of ya?" asked Red.

"That's it, in a nutshell," said Jumpy, and the rest nodded, fervently.

"Jasus, Po, did ya hear anything like that before?" said Red, turning to Po and fighting hard to keep a straight face.

"Unbelievable, just unbelievable, Jasus, that's some story, all right. What de ya think, Red?"

"I agree. Ya know, what happened here is that yis annoyed, or pissed off, or awakened a spirit in the graveyard for some reason and it decided to get ya. Yis were very lucky ta get away, ya know. Yis could just as easy been dragged inta a grave."

"We know," came the combined answer.

Later Red and Po were lying on their beds, talking.

"Another historical moment created," mused Po.

"What are ya talkin' about?"

"First time in the history of the world that a ghost was scared by a ghost."

The two roared with laughter, ending up with Red falling off the bed.

End

Home Again

1961

Anto and his Uncle Roberto, were waiting at Edward Street Railway Station when Red and Po finally arrived 30 minutes late, from Dublin. Both hauling suitcases and bags and wearing broad smiles.

"Welcome back, shitheads," smiled Anto.

"Well, fartface. You've actually got uglier," answered Po.

"Now, Po, that's not very nice. Ya should never talk ta mentally disabled people like that," added Red.

When all the hugs, handshakes, punches, hair rubs and greetings were over Roberto drove the two home to discard their luggage, say their hellos to family and then on to Uncle Luigi's Café, their home away from home.

"Ah, the travellers return," greeted a toothless, grinning Uncle Luigi, from behind the counter.

"Sit, sit. You must eat after long journey. I make very special pasta for you."

Fifteen minutes later, Red and Po were tucking into a huge pasta dinner prepared by Uncle Luigi, himself.

"So, tell me all the news," said Anto, sliding into the snug beside Red.

"Tell him all the news, Po."

"You tell him all the friggin' news, I'm busy."

"I see he hasn't changed a'tall," laughed Anto.

"Naw, he's still a shithead. Any news here?" Red managed ta get out of a full mouth of pasta.

"Trish Jennings is pregnant."

"Shit. Wee Trish Jennings, who to?"

"No one knows for sure, but the bets are on Marty Havern."

"She was goin' out with him, I remember."

"Well, the book's still open, but Marty is two ta one on."

"Not worth a bet."

"But, ya never know. Rumours have it that your man, Humpy Clark, was seen with her."

"No way, she at least has a little taste. She wouldn't be seen dead with that creep."

"Women are funny creatures. Who knows what they would do next."

"De ya hear the voice of experience?" laughed Po.

"Shut up beanhead," snarled Anto.

When they had finished and all the tummy rubs, burps, and stretching were over and done with, important things had to be discussed.

"So, who's datin' who, Anto, and who's been fightin' with who, and what scandal have ya?"

"Let's see. Well, ya know Francie McCall, from Church Street, well wasn't he only caught breakin' into a garage on the Rathfriland Road, with Dumpy Collins."

"Holy shit, who caught them?" asked Po.

"Cops were passin' and saw their flashlight, so they did."

"Jasus, that was a bit of bad luck, for sure," commented Red.

"They were up at court yesterday before that auld bastard of a judge, Parrot nose Wyllie. It appears Francie was up twice before the auld dick, and he got four months in the Crumlin."

"Holy shit, that was a bit rough. How did Dumpy do?" asked Red.

"Fined £150 and bound over ta keep the peace for 12 months."

"Four friggin' months in the Crum, how long will he have ta do?" asked Po.

"Well, with remission, he'll be out in three months," said Anto.

"Still, three months in that friggin' place. Christ, a wouldn't even put Morgan in there," smiled Po, nodding toward Red.

Red just pulled a face.

"Can't remember the guy your woman's bin datin' Po. His name will come ta me in a minute," said Anto, rubbing his chin wistfully.

"You're such a smart arse, Falsoni. My woman is totally out of her head crazy about me, so she is," replied Po angrily.

"Well now, Po, a have ta say, ya were close there, ya got it half right. Your woman is totally out of her head crazy all right. After all, isn't she goin' out with you?" smiled Red.

"Surrounded by total shitheads, so I am. God hates me, I'm convinced of that."

"Well, sure the poor man's only goin' along with the majority," said Red, seriously.

This got Red a sharp kick on the shin, which he didn't appreciate.

Over the next hour the gang were arriving in ones and twos, until they were all there. They all stayed until closing and when all the customers had left and the floor was washed, tables cleaned and the place looking spick and span, Uncle Luigi came out from behind the counter.

"Boys, keep the quiet now. To welcome you all a'home, I have opened some'a nice a Canti for you."

Anto had already begun pouring the wine into the glasses he had been laying on the counter. There was a round of applause and cheering from all, which was quickly hushed by Luigi.

"Keep the quiet boys, the police will hear and want to come in for some, too," said Luigi, with his usual toothless grin. "Oh, before I go, now you all know how to make'a the coats, you make' a one for Luigi," said the still grinning Luigi, as he left.

An important and somewhat exciting episode in the boy's lives was over. They had experienced life in the big city, dated girls, explored Dublin, played football against the Dublin factory workers, and ended up winning 10 games to 7, and were now expert coat makers. Dunno almost walked in front of a bus but was grabbed in time by Bishop who has never allowed him to forget how he had risked his life to save him. Jumpy had his first bath in six months by falling into the Tolka River. Red and Bishop raided the fridge in the middle of the night and ate a full carton of ice cream. They convinced Po that he had been sleep-walking and had eaten the ice cream. They did it so well, he actually believed them.

As for the company they were working for in Dublin, they got large grants from the government to open the factory in Newry. Just over a year later, the General Manager disappeared with quite a large bankroll and the factory closed.

The Easter Egg

1961

Red, Po, Anto and Topcoat were sitting and talking in Uncle Luigi's. It was Good Friday, and Po was worried about getting an Easter egg for his girlfriend, Trish.

"She likes chocolate, so she does, but a don't know what type of egg ta get, ya see," said Po.

"All the stupid things are chocolate anyway, so what's the problem?" asked Topcoat.

"It's the size of the egg a have ta think about, ya see, and whether it should be one of them ones in a basket."

"Jasus, help us," said Red, putting his face in his hands.

"It's all right for yous, so it is. I've never had ta buy an egg for a girlfriend before."

"Ah, ya poor, wee man, sure the stress ya must be under, a understand, so a do. Ya know a lesser man would buckle under the weight," said Anto, with a straight face.

"Anto, go screw yourself."

"Jasus, de ya hear that? That's the thanks ya get for bein' kind and understandin' and carin' and helpful, and . . . shit, I've run out, help me Red."

"Christian?"

"There ya go, Christian. Thanks Red."

"No bother a'tall, Anto. Total pleasure ta be of assistance ta ya."

"Ya see, Po. I'm trying ta do my level best to help your wee self through this terrible dilemma," said Anto.

"Po, for a girlfriend ya have ta get an egg in a basket. It's traditional," said Red.

"Are ya sure?" asked Po.

"Sure, I'm sure."

"Don't listen ta him, Po. What ya want ta get is one of them eggs that comes with a cuddly toy, like a teddy bear," pointed out Anto.

"A teddy bear?"

"A teddy bear."

"Yeah, that's all right Po, but they're more for a wee girl, ya know? Not like a girl ya've been trying ta get the knickers off," said Red.

"I'd have ta go with Red there, Po. I would go with the basket. Much classier altogether," added Topcoat.

"I was leanin' towards a basket, my own self this couple of days," replied Po.

"Leanin' towards a basket? Po, you've been a basket case for years," put in Red.

"You're a whore, Morgan, de ya know that?" snarled Po.

This was almost drowned out by the laughter of his companions.

"Right, that's it. I'm gettin' a basket, so I am."

"They have them over in Quinn's the Milestone, so they have, Po," added Jumpy.

"Jumpy, now don't start being silly now. Po wants a real chocolate egg, not an auld imitation one," said Red, seriously.

"A real one?" replied Jumpy.

"Of course, a real one."

"What de ya mean, a real one?"

At this point the rest of the lads at the table knew Jumpy was about to get taken for a ride, big time. Red was off and running.

"A real one Jumpy is not a chocolate egg made in a factory, but, a for real, laid, chocolate egg."

"Laid chocolate egg, ya mean by a chicken?"

"What else?"

"You're off your head," smiled Jumpy.

"Now Jumpy, please don't be tellin' me ya have never heard of an Easter Chicken?"

"What's that?"

Red looked around the table. "Isn't it terrible the lack of knowledge some people have these days?"

"Terrible, awful," said Anto.

"Total disgrace," said Topcoat.

"Somethin' should be done about it," added Po.

"Hold on a minute Red. Are ya trying ta tell me that there are Easter Chickens?"

"Of course there are Easter Chickens. Specially bred, just for Easter."

"Bred for what?"

"Jumpy, are ya listenin' a'tall? For their eggs, of course."

"A don't understand?"

"Look, these chickens are fed sugar and cocoa instead of the normal chicken food, ya see. So instead of layin' normal eggs, they lay chocolate eggs."

"Don't be stupid, Red."

"Jasus, will ya tell him, Anto, for God's sake?"

"He's right, Jumpy. That's what happens, ok."

"That's crap, chickens layin' chocolate eggs. De ya think I'm an ejit, altogether?" laughed Jumpy.

"Jumpy, you being a ejit has nothin' ta do with it."

"Chickens layin' Easter eggs?" laughed Jumpy.

"What can a tell ya, that's what they do."

"But, sure most Easter eggs are big for God's sake, not the size laid by chickens."

"Jumpy, did a not tell ya they were special chickens, not your everyday cluck cluckin' yokes."

"You're sayin' they're big yokes?"

"Big?" laughed Red looking around the table. "Tell him, Topcoat."

"Jasus, big they are for sure, like ostriches, so they are."

"That's what I was gonna say, so it is," added Anto.

Jumpy called Shifty McShane, who was on his way out of the café.

"Shifty, is there such a thing as Easter Chickens?"

Shifty caught Red's almost imperceptible nod.

"Of course, everyone knows about Easter Chickens," answered Shifty, as he continued on his way.

"There, see?" said Po.

"Well I didn't know, did I?" said Jumpy defensively.

"Well, ya know now, don't ya? I'm here ta improve your education, so I am, Jumpy," added Red, patting Jumpy on the shoulder.

"Red, Po, will ya give me a wee hand with somethin'?" said Anto, sliding out of the snug.
Both followed him to the kitchen.
"I have a plan."
Red looked at Po.
"Now there's an unusual thing, Po."
"Very rare, for sure."
"Shut up will yis, and listen," said Anto, seriously.
"Now, ya know every Easter Sunday mornin' we go up Courtney Hill for the rollin' of the eggs and a bit of craic?" went on Anto.
"Yeah?"
"And we do the egg eatin' contest?"
"I remember, ya made a wee clean-up last year on bets," laughed Po.
"Naw, just a couple of bob. But, I've come up with a new one, depending on 'Brains' here, if he can make it," said Anto, nodding at Po.
"Ok, tell us," said Po, sitting down.
"Ok, now Po, would it be possible ta make a wee hole in an egg without it being seen?"
"A real egg?"
"Yeah."
"Well, I suppose it's possible, why?"
"And would it be possible ta make the shell harder so it won't crack?"
"Suppose. Will ya tell me what you're up ta, will ya?"
"Right, now suppose an egg was ten times heavier than a normal egg. Would ya be able ta throw it further?"
"Of course ya would, what are ya gettin' at?"
"This year, instead of an egg eatin' competition, we will have an egg, throwin' competition."
"Egg throwin'?" puzzled Red.
"I see what he's at. We fix our own egg ta be heavier so we'll be certain ta win," smiled Po.
"That wee man's a genius, Red."
"Yeah, when he's sleepin'."
"Will ya do it, Po?"
"Now hold on a wee minute. I take it you're running a book on this egg throwin' thing?"

"That's the idea."
"And, how much do I get?"
"We get?" put in Red.
"How does fifty fifty sound?"
Red and Po exchanged glances, and the deal was done.

After using up a number of eggs, Po was eventually able to extract the inside of the egg through a small circular hole. He replaced the egg innards with a fine sand. He then filled the hole in the shell with putty. When the putty was dry and hardened the next day, the egg had a face painted on it, totally covering the putty. This was now a tradition for the egg rolling, some had faces, others, designs. There was a prize for the best decorated egg. Po painted a hardening glue over the shell to make it a lot less breakable.

*   *   *

Everyone had gathered at a steep grassy incline just off Courtney Hill for the traditional egg rolling. This went on for some time, and there were lots of prizes for the kids. Anto had already told everyone about the 'Egg Throwing Competition'. Almost all the gang entered.
"Now, this is the starting point," said Anto, pointing at a coat lying on the ground.
"I will be the judge, along with Red here, to see whose egg is thrown the longest distance. First prize will be a half crown. Will the first thrower get ready. Red will take note of the throwers here and make sure everything is done right. I will be at the other end ta mark the distance of the eggs."

When everything was ready, the first thrower lined up and threw his egg. It landed about 30 feet away. This was average for most of them. That is, of course, except Po. His egg travelled twice the distance of most of the others. When all the eggs were thrown, everyone ran to see where his egg had landed and to reclaim it. Po was of course declared the winner.
"Hold on a minute, here," said Ginger.
"How come Po's egg went so far? Somethin's fishy here. Let's see that egg, Po."
Po handed his egg to Ginger.
Red looked at Anto, who seemed to have lost the colour in his face.

Ginger shook the egg, tapped it, and a piece of the shell came off exposing a normal boiled egg inside.

"Are ya happy now, Ginger? An' you've only gone an' ruined my lovely egg."

"Sorry about that Po."

An hour later Red, Po, and Anto were out the back of the café.

"Ok, how the frig did ya do it, ya wee smart, intelligent, genius person?" laughed Anto.

"Well, a was thinkin', ya see, what if anythin' went wrong? So, a boiled a second egg, painted the same face on it, and kept it in ma pocket. When we all ran ta where our eggs landed, I did a quick swap with the one in ma pocket."

"Jasus Red, this wee man is out there on his own so he is."

"Taught him all he knows," smiled Red.

"That wasn't too much," smirked Po.

"Ah, but ya see Po, a taught ya all ya know, but a didn't teach ya all I know," smiled Red patting the side of his nose with his finger.

Anto divided up the winnings taken on bets and on entry fees. That night all three went to the Savoy cinema to see a re-run of an old Irving Berlin movie, ironically called, Easter Parade.

End

Do You Know Where You Are?

1963

"Where did ya get the car?" asked Po as he reached the driver's window of the Ford Popular that had stopped to his hails on Hill Street.

"Uncle Tommy loaned it to me. He's away ta Wales for a week and asked me ta look after the car," answered Red.

"Jasus, he's nuts and you're lucky," smiled Po.

"Fancy goin' for a wee spin?" asked Red.

There was no answer from Po. Within ten seconds he was sitting in the passenger seat.

"Let's go then."

"Where will we go?" asked Red.

"Let's go up by the Flagstaff and down into Omeath."

"Sounds good ta me. It'll be dark in about 30 minutes. I like the Flagstaff at night. All the lights in Warrenpoint and around the coast are really beautiful."

Red drove along Hill Street and turned right towards Dublin Bridge where he had to stop to allow the Warrenpoint train to cross at the Level Crossing. The street filled up quickly with steam from the coal powered engine as the train slowed to stop at Dublin Bridge Station. The Level Crossing gates began to open and two young boys jumped aboard for the free ride.

"You used to do that all the time," said Red smiling.

"Do what?"

"Stand on the railway gates ta get a wee spin. Ah, sure God love ya."

"Piss off ya creep, you did it too so ya did."

"Sure a did, but not when a was fifteen."

"I'm not answerin' ya. You're just tryin' ta get a rise outta me so ya are."

"More than wee Marian could do I'm told," laughed Red.

This earned him a hard punch on the bicep, which made him wince.

A few minutes later they were going under Cloughue Railway Bridge, a massive granite structure affording the Belfast to Dublin train to cross the main Dublin Road. They were now just two miles from the border with the South of Ireland. Just after they passed under the bridge they came to a large British Army Checkpoint where they had to stop and have their identification and car checked. A British Soldier who had been talking to the driver in front of them approached their car. Red wound down the window.

"Evening gentlemen, sorry for the delay."

"No problem," answered Red.

"Is that a Manchester United badge you're wearing?"

"That it is," smiled Red holding up his coat lapel.

"Nice one, I'm from Manchester, but I'm the Black Sheep in our house for supporting Man U. My dad and all my brothers support the Blues."

"Well, sure it just goes ta show ya, we can't all be intelligent," Red smiled.

The soldier roared laughing.

"Love it, I'm going to say that next time I write home."

The soldier at the head of the queue shouted something and waved them forward.

"They're ok, I checked them."

They were waved straight through and continued on their way.

"Jasus that was close so it was," said Red.

"What was?" asked Po.

"We were lucky he didn't ask you who you supported, Jasus, if ya had a said Aston Villa, we could have been there all night. Everyone knows they are a load of crap and their supporters are all brainless hooligans, the soldiers would have labelled ya right away as a terrorist for sure," smiled Red.

"You're such a smart mouth Morgan. Ya didn't have a lot ta say when we beat yis 2 – 0 in the FA Cup Final a couple a years ago did ya?"

"Everyone is entitled ta a little luck once in their lives, that was theirs. I hope yis enjoyed it cause it will never happen again."

"That's what you think," smirked Po.

They turned left just before the Customs Post towards the Flagstaff View Point. Within five minutes they were standing on a small wall in the car park gazing at the wonderful view of the coastline below stretching from Warrenpoint, through Rostrevor and Kilowen to Greencastle.

"Aren't the lights great?" commented Po lighting up a Gallagher's Blue cigarette.

"Love this view. Even during the day it's fantastic."

"Yeah, ya can see the Mourne Mountains great from here, ya can even see Cloughmore Stone so ya can."

When they had finished two cigarettes they began the second part of their outing to Omeath Village. Just outside the entrance to Flagstaff View Point, they turned right, down the steep hill toward Omeath. Red knew this road very well and knew it was both twisty and dangerous so made sure he drove slowly. Suddenly he noticed a red light flashing at him about a hundred yards ahead.

"Customs?" asked Po.

"No, I think it's the Brits," replied Red as he slowed the car to a stop. He was right, it was the British Army doing 'Vehicle Spot Checks'. Red wound down his window. The camouflaged face of a soldier appeared. They were all carrying guns.

"Turn off your engine please," said the soldier.

Red did so.

"Where are you coming from?"

"Newry," answered Red.

"And you are going to?"

"Omeath."

"Strange way to go from Newry to Omeath?"

"Just havin' a spin. We were at the Flagstaff."

"Really, step out of the car please."

Red and Po did as they were told.

"Licence?" asked the soldier.

Red reached into his pocket and produced his Driving Licence. At the other side of the car Po was being asked for identification also, for which he had none.

"Open the boot please," requested the first soldier.

Red took the keys out of the ignition and walked to the rear of the car. He opened the boot and the soldier began searching inside. The other soldier was searching inside the car.

"Come around here," said the soldier to Red bringing him back to the driver's door.

"Place your hands on the roof."

Red did so. He was patted down from head to toe very professionally.

"Ok, stay here please," said the soldier as he walked toward another soldier a few yards along the road who was, it appeared to Red, to be an officer. He shined his torch on what appeared to be Red's Licence and mumbled something to another soldier who appeared to be carrying a large radio on his back. A few minutes later the soldier returned to Red and called Po to the driver's side of the car.

"You do know you should not under any circumstances be travelling without identification don't you?" he said to Po.

"Yeah, I know, I just never thought of it tonight. Comin' up here was a sort of spur of the moment thing."

Red was looking around the area in the now quickly failing light getting his bearings and with a slight quizzical look on his face.

"Ah, I see, a Man U fan are we?" smiled the soldier.

"I am indeed," smiled Red.

"You too?" he said looking at Po.

"No way, Villa."

"Well good man yourself. I've supported Villa all my life, and here I am in the very home town of Peter McParland who smashed the United nets twice to win us the FA Cup."

"Best moments of my life," smiled Po.

"Nothing to say Mr. Man United?" the soldier smiled at Red.

"I prefer not ta talk about depressin' moments in ma life," said Red with a straight face.

"On you go. Drive carefully," smiled the soldier.

Red and Po got into the car and continued their journey.

"Nice guy that soldier. Some of them can be real shits," said Po.

Red braked suddenly and looked around.

"What's wrong?"

"Holy shit, tell ya in a minute," said Red turning the car on the narrow road and starting back up the hill to where the soldiers were. As he neared them he saw the red light inviting him to stop. He opened his window as a soldier approached."

"Hi, I just came through here a minute ago, could a talk to the soldier that stopped us please?"

The soldier called out and another soldier approached the car, it was the one who had talked to them earlier."

"Hello again," he said bending down.

"Hello again," smiled Red, "Ok if I get out a second?"

"Sure," said the soldier opening the driver's door for him. When Red got out he asked if he could have a word with the officer, who was called and promptly arrived.

"Hello," said Red.

"Hello Sir, is there a problem?"

"Well, yes, I'm afraid there is and I just thought I had better tell ya about it. Now, don't take this the wrong way, but do you know where you are?"

The officer and the soldier exchanged glances.

"What do you mean?" asked the officer.

"I mean, do you know, exactly where you are?"

"You mean, map reference? Yes, I do, why?"

"Well Sir, ya see, I know this area very well, come here a lot durin' the summer. Now back up the road there ya'll see a wee stream goin' under the road, about a half a mile back a would say."

"Yes, noticed it, what about it?"

"Well, I think your map reader is in a wee bit of trouble. That stream is actually the border and yis are about a half a mile inside the Republic of Ireland."

"What? Sergeant bring the map here, on the double."

The map arrived and was examined closely by the officer and a number of soldiers under their torch lights. A few minutes later the officer approached Red.

"I can't thank you enough for coming back to tell us our position. You are of course correct, we have inadvertently strayed over the border. We will remedy that immediately. Once again, thank you very much. If you ever find yourself having any problems contact me," said the officer handing Red a card.

"Thank you, hope I will never need to contact you," laughed Red.

Ten minutes later they pulled up at the pier in Omeath Village.
"Well, now wasn't that somethin'?" said Po.
"That it was, but only to be expected I suppose," said Red seriously.
"What do ya mean?"
"Well them gettin' lost and all."
"Why was it ta be expected?"
"Ah Po, for Christ's sake, don't be stupid. Sure wasn't your man an Aston Villa supporter for God's sake?"
Po's reply was language that could be expected from Villa supporters.

End

The Surprise Party

1963

The gang were engaged in a secret meeting, that afternoon, out back of Uncle Luigi's. Anto had called this secret meeting of the complete gang, secret in the sense that the only one being kept in the dark about it was Red, as the meeting was in fact about him. The following Thursday was his eighteenth birthday and Anto, Po and the gang wanted to make sure it would be a memorable one.

"Well, if I ask them, I can't see any problem. They all know Red and would not charge for the use of the hall," said Po.

"Ok then, The Bucket it is, then. We'll leave that end of things to your own self, Po. Now, we will need music. Anybody got any ideas?"

"Can I suggest that group Glen Harris has, The Flavours? I know Glen well, and I think I might be able to get him to do it reasonably cheap," suggested the Bishop.

"Great. Then that will be your job, Bishop. You'll be in charge of the entertainment. Now what about eats? We'll need some food. I will organise sandwiches. What else de ya think?"

"Why don't we all ask our moms to bake somethin'? That way we will have a good range of stuff," suggested Shifty McShane.

"He's right. That's a very good idea, so it is," commented Po.

"I agree," said Jumpy. "My mom makes great apple tarts."

"So yous got the electric in then Jumpy?" smiled Jammy.

"Jasus, you're so funny McAteer," snapped Jumpy.

"I was just askin', for God's sake," replied Jammy, winking at Anto.

"Well then, are we all organised?" asked Po.

"We are, but there is one last thing. What about presents? Now as I see it, we can all buy him a present individually, or if we all put our money together, we could get him something really fantastic. What do ya think?" asked Anto.

"I think poolin' our money is, by far, the best idea," commented the Bishop.

There was a general agreement among the gathering. The secret meeting had ended.

*   *   *

"Hi, shithead."

Red turned to see a smiling Po approaching him in Newry Market.

"Well, if it isn't short arse, his own self."

"What's happenin'?"

"Frig all, just gettin' a cabbage for granny. What ya up ta?"

"Not a lot. So, in five days ya will be a big 18?"

"So?"

"Well, since I am older than ya, and am already 18, I would be only too willin' to give ya the benefit of my vast experience, bein' an adult, ya see. I mean, that's what friends are for, ya know."

"Ya know what, Po? You are a walking advertisement for Aspirin."

"Now ya see, even though you're so close ta bein' a grown up, ya still behave in childish ways."

"If ya don't shut up, ya better have a likin' for hospital food!"

"Jasus, ya'r such a smart arse, aren't ya? Let me tell ya, being an adult, like me, is not as easy as I make it look, ya know."

"Po, ya do know that ya need your wee head examined, don't ya? You are exactly two months older than me. Two months, for Christ's sake. Ta hear ya, people would think ya were years older."

"There ya go, ya see. Ya know nothin'. It's not a time thing, can't ya understand. Time doesn't come into it, it's more . . . experience. More being grown up, more mental, ya see."

"Ya'r right. Friggin' mental is the right description for ya."

"Now ya don't have ta worry or be upset now, Red. Ya can depend on your very best friend in the world ta help ya through the trauma of growin' up."

"Jasus, I need this on a Saturday mornin'," Red mumbled, almost to himself.

"Now first of all, have ya got your clothes, yet?"

"Clothes?"

"Jasus, you're useless. How can ya turn into a man on Thursday and still be wearin' wee boys clothes? Ya will have ta go and get some money and buy some adult clothes and stuff. Jasus, where's your head at anyway. Sure, ya can't be runnin' around dressed like that when ya'r a man, ya know."

"Po, the time has come for you to shut your face. Ya'r beginnin' ta get on my nerves, right about now."

"This jeans and sweatshirt thing will have ta go, ya know. Proper trousers and shirt and tie will be required, ya see. Women will be lookin' at ya in a different way now that you're a man."

Red stepped back and examined Po from head to toe.

"I see. Jeans, stupid T shirt, shoes that went out of style in the 1800's. Yeah, I can see you're wearin' the very grown up clothin'."

"Morgan, have ya no cop on a'tall? I dressed like this so as not ta make ya look bad."

"Jasus help me . . ."

"Now a want ya ta listen very careful ta this, right?"

"What now?"

"Next Thursday, which I got from a good source, is your birthday."

"Jasus, Po, how did ya find that out? Sure you're a genuine miniature Private Detective."

Po patted the side of his nose with his finger.

"I have my sources, and don't even think of torture. I would die before I would give them up."

"I would be into torturin' ya, just for the sheer pleasure of it."

"Now, listen. I have a birthday present organised for ya."

"Go on."

"Now it took a lot of blood, sweat and tears, not forgettin' pain, lack of sleep, nervous tension, great expense, hard work, and . . . . ."

"Jasus would ya shut up and tell me?"

"I am taking ya somewhere, at my expense."

"Where?"

"That's the big surprise. Ya will love it."

"Where?"

"Can't tell ya. Would only spoil it for ya."

"Well, I'm goin' nowhere anyways. I was supposed ta be going out with Maureen but she cancelled. Some stupid family thing."

"Well there ya go, then. We're all set."

"Suppose."

*   *   *

Thursday night arrived and Po called to Red's house, as arranged, after seven.

Po stopped and examined Red, in the hallway.

"A thought a told ya ta get dressed up ya lump?"

Red was wearing a new three piece navy suit bought for him as a present by his mom and dad. A lovely blue, button down collared shirt, and an expensive looking tie.

"I'm havin' fantasies of your face and my fist havin' an accident," snarled Red.

"Suppose ya will have ta do, come on."

Po turned right outside Red's front door.

"Where are we goin'?"

"Will ya hold your wilt, will ya? Ya'll find out soon enough."

In fact, Red would find out a lot sooner than even he thought. His house was only five hundred yards from 'The Bucket'.

As Po turned into the entrance steps to The Bucket, Red stopped.

"We're goin' ta the friggin' Bucket?"

"No, ya weirdo, just have to call in for a minute ta see someone."

Red accepted the explanation and followed Po up the entrance steps.

"Did I ever tell ya . . . Jasus, ya have a lovely arse?"

"No ya fruit, ya didn't."

"Good, I hate tellin' lies."

"Every fruit in the town fancies me, I'll have ya know," said Po, over his shoulder.

"Yeah, a heard. The word's got around. Ya must be good, right enough."

"Shut your face, ya friggin', bastardin' whore."

They had reached the top of the steps and Po pushed Red in first.

"Hello you."

Red spun around to see his girlfriend Maureen standing behind the door smiling. She was dressed in his favourite red dress and looked radiant.

"What . . . ?"

She arrived beside him and led him into the hall. As they walked through the door there was a deafening burst of sound as a band and fifty people began singing 'Happy Birthday'. Red stopped in astonishment and looked around. He turned and looked at Po.

"See you, you're dead."

Red turned and looked at a singing smiling Maureen, "and so are you."

A great time was had by all. Near the end of the night Red was pushed, dragged and almost carried to the stage. The band leader spoke, "Ladies and scruffs."

There was hissing and booing.

"On this auspicious . . ." There was loud applause.

"I didn't get much schoolin', but I met the scholars comin' out."

This also got loud applause.

"On this auspicious occasion, we are gathered here tonight to celebrate Red Morgan's eighteenth birthday." This was followed by loud applause and cheering.

"Red has graced us by being here with all his friends. That's Po there and the drunk guy in the toilet." More cheering and laughter.

"It's my pleasure to present him with a small present on behalf of all his many friends."

Red was handed a wrapped package, about nine inches long, and encouraged to open it. He did so, and produced a very large carrot! The crowd roared, at both the carrot and the expression on Red's face.

"Now," laughed the band leader, "look inside the carrot, Red."

Red looked puzzled. He looked at the carrot and noticed it had a cut around the middle. Breaking it in two halves he noticed it had been hollowed out and there was something inside wrapped in plastic. Encouraged to continue, he unwrapped it and took out what appeared to be Flight Tickets.

"Well, read them out to us, Red," said the band leader.

Red opened the tickets . . .

"Jasus . . ."

The crowd roared with laughter.

"They're tickets for a weekend in Manchester," mumbled Red.

The crowd applauded. The band leader using his hands hushed everyone. He reached inside his pocket and produced another envelope.

"I'm afraid there wasn't enough room in the carrot for this," he said, handing it to Red.

Red fumbled with the envelope until he managed to get it open. He slid out two red tickets.

"Oh my God . . ." Red managed to get out.

"Tell us all what it is, Red," said the band leader.

"Two tickets . . . to . . . Old Trafford . . . to see Man United playin' Liverpool."

The hall erupted with cheering.

Later, Red was getting a sandwich, when Maureen slid in beside him.

"Hi you."

"You knew about this, didn't ya?"

"No, I didn't. I knew they had something special for ya, but they wouldn't trust me, in case I told ya."

"Now, this gives me a really big problem."

"What's that?"

"Who will I take with me? Can't make up my mind. Po, or maybe Anto or Jumpy?"

Maureen grabbed him by the lapels and she spoke through gritted teeth.

"What did ya say?"

"A was just sayin' that a think me an you will have a great time."

They both laughed and hugged.

Next day, Po found Red sitting in Uncle Luigi's, reading the paper. He slid into the snug opposite him.

"Well, ya had a great night last night."

"Best night I ever had in my life," smiled Red. "An' a know you had a lot ta do with it."

Po blushed and looked down.

"Ah sure, it was just a tiny wee part I played."

"Well, whatever your part, thanks."

Red stood up to leave.

"Have a few things ta do for mom, see ya later."

"Later."

Red walked a few steps, stopped, and returned to the snug.

"And Po, see next year, try and get the date right," said Red, as he turned and walked toward the door.

"Hang on. Wait, ya bastard," Po shouted, as he raced after him.

They were now on the street and Red was doing his best to ignore Po.

"What de ya mean by that?"

"By what?"

"Ya know friggin' well. The date thing."

"Ah the date. Yes. Well, sure ya got it wrong."

"What ya talkin' about?"

"Ma birthday."

"What are ya talkin' about, got it wrong?"

"Ya got the date wrong. My birthday wasn't yesterday."

"You are a lying, bastard."

"Whatever ya think."

"I know for sure it was your birthday yesterday."

"Who told ya?"

"You did. Your mom did."

"My mom always gets me mixed up with my Uncle Pajoe. And as for me? I tell lies. Don't like all the fuss."

"You're a lying, whore, fruit, bastardin' friggin' shithead."

"Ya still got it wrong."

"I friggin' didn't."

"Did."

"Didn't."

"Did."

"Ok, bastard, when is it then?"

"It's . . . can't tell ya."

"Whore."

End

The Border House Inn

1964

Red was sitting in the first snug in Uncle Luigi's, chatting to Anto, when Po arrived.

"Well?" said Po, sitting down. "What's happenin'?"

"I was just tellin' Anto here, that if he were ta go back ta school, pass a few exams, raise his IQ sort of thing, he would be able ta support Man United instead of Liverpool."

"That's a very good idea, but if both of ya were to get a likin' for football, I could manage ta get yis an Aston Villa scarf, each."

"Jasus, de ya hear your man? It's because I like football that I don't support Villa in the first place, or for that matter, Liverpool. Now if I was feelin' a bit down and a bit depressed, or somethin', I'd watch a Villa or a Pool game ta cheer myself up. Sure, it's better than watchin' a comedy."

"You're a real smart arse, Morgan. Anyway, let me tell yis my news. I heard this mornin' that my cousin Bob, from London, is comin' over next weekend, with his wife. I have been ordered ta take them out one of the nights he will be here. Have yous any ideas?"

"Wow, let's see, now. Ya need ta take him somewhere up-market, I would think. Him bein' from London, and all that. I know, take him out for a meal ta a top of the range restaurant," suggested Anto.

"That would be a bit on the expensive side, wouldn't it?" asked Po.

"Not a'tall. Not a bit of it. I'll even put on a clean tablecloth for yis," smiled Anto.

"Hilarious. Now will yis help me out here, will yis?"

"Take them out for a drink?" suggested Red.

"I was thinkin' that, me own self. But where?"

"Somewhere where there's music. Irish Music would be a good idea, specially for visitors," said Red.

"Brilliant! That would be perfect. Where's the best pub for Irish Music at the weekends?"

"Most of the pubs in the town have music, but Irish, not sure," mused Anto.

"Got it!" smiled Red, slapping the table, "The Border House Inn."

"The Border House Inn?" said Po.

"The very one. Was thinkin' that, meself," smiled Red.

"Will ya stop messin'. Why the Border House Inn?"

"Great tourist pub. They'll love it. Great Irish Music, too."

"Anto, have ya the paper, so we can see who's on next weekend."

Anto got up and left the snug in search of the Newry Reporter. He returned a few minutes later, reading the entertainment section.

"It's the 'Rebel Sound' that's playin'."

"They're very good, Po. Well worth seein'," said Red, seriously.

"Yea, know them. They're good. That's where we'll go, then."

"We?" said Red.

"Well, yous are goin' too. Ya didn't expect me ta go on ma own, did ya? See yis later," said Po, as he left the snug quickly.

Red and Anto looked at each other.

"Ya doin' anythin' at the weekend, Red?"

"Was thinkin' a goin' ta the Border House Inn. Wanna come?"

"Love ta."

Po's relatives arrived, and on the night they were all going out together, they met up in Uncle Luigi's.

"Bob, Mary, this is my worst friend, Red, and this is some guy called Anto, who just hangs around us."

They both laughed and shook hands with Red and Anto. Bob was tall and well built, in his middle forties. Mary was rather petite, quite pretty, and perhaps a few years younger than her husband.

"Bob, I know there's no need for me ta tell ya about Po. He tells lies, is insanely jealous of both Anto and myself because of our good looks, charm, and warm personalities. He also supports Aston Villa. Enough said," commented Red, seriously.

Both Bob and Mary laughed loudly.

"I'll tell Roberto we are ready ta go," said Anto, turning and walking toward the kitchen.

"Roberto?" Bob asked Po.

"That's Anto's uncle. He is drivin' us ta the pub, and pickin' us up later. It's about ten miles away. Just on the border, in South Armagh. We all want ta have a drink, and sure, ya couldn't chance drivin' with a drink in ya, out there. The place is hivin' with cops."

"Ah, understand."

When they were on their way, Bob spoke to Roberto.

"It's very kind of you to take us to the pub."

"No problem a'tall. It was a simple choice. Do this little trip or get nagged for a week from your man there. The pizza burner."

"Jasus, ya make one mistake and never hear the end of it," moaned Anto.

"He burned a pizza, Roberto?" asked Red.

"Burned would be an understatement. Cremated would be a better word."

"Really, Mr. Chef of the year, huh?"

"Did he tell ya that?"

"Sure, he's always boastin' about how good a cook he is. Isn't that right, Po?"

"Never shuts up about it."

"Go ahead, why don't yis just talk among yourselves, like I'm not here," complained Anto.

"See, now you've gone and hurt his feelin's, Roberto," said Po.

"Will you lot give it a rest, will yis?"

"Now Anto, don't be like that. I can understand how devastated ya must have been, burnin' a pizza an all. Probably scarred ya mentally," said Red.

"That's what it did, all right, scarred him mentally. Sure, ya can see it lookin' at him so ya can," added Po.

"We don't need to go out to the pub for entertainment. We are getting great entertainment right here, in the car," laughed Mary.

"Talkin' of the pub, we are here," said Roberto. "Give me a ring when yis are ready ta come home."

The pub was quite big, with two lounges, two bars and a restaurant. When they got inside, the 'Rebel Sound' were in full swing, with the crowd singing along. They found an empty table, and Bob insisted on going for the drinks. Red offered to help. While they were waiting at the bar, Bob nodded towards the floor.

"What's that big yellow line for?" he asked.

"Ah, forgot ta tell ya about that. Ya see, when the English, in all their wisdom, drew up the border between Northern and Southern Ireland, their border came right through the centre of this pub and right through the car park."

"Are you serious?"

"Very. Now this is what happens. We are now in Northern Ireland, right? Now the bar closes at eleven thirty, with thirty minutes drinkin' up time. We all get up and go into the other lounge, on the other side of the yellow line, as does the band. Then we will be in the South of Ireland where the bar can stay open until one thirty."

"This is totally unbelievable," laughed Bob.

"Welcome ta Ireland," laughed Red.

Bob and Mary were having a great time singing along with the band, and even getting up a few times on the dance floor, to try out an Irish jig or hornpipe.

The band finished playing and the lead singer announced, "Thank you ladies and the rest of yis," to loud boos.

"I have to now tell ya all, that we were so disappointed by our audience tonight, that we are all deeply depressed and heartbroken." This got a chorus of 'Ahhh's' from the crowd.

"Therefore, we have all decided, there is no other course for us but to pack up our gear and leave the country." This got loud cheers.

"We are moving to the South of Ireland, where we know we will get a better audience."

"Is this where we move, Red?" asked Bob.

"Yeah, this is it. Let's just take our drinks now, and go ta make sure we get decent seats."

They all began moving towards the back lounge. As they crossed the yellow line Po said in a loud voice, "Welcome to the Republic of Ireland."

Anto rang Roberto when it was time to go home, and arranged to meet him outside. Later when they were all in the car, and on their way home, Bob and Mary were still singing Irish Rebel songs.

"A see yis enjoyed yourselves," said Roberto, laughing.

"Enjoyed ourselves? Roberto, it was the best night out ever, and the most unusual that we ever had, in our lives. I can tell you we will never forget it," laughed Bob.

"Did yis tell them the story of Willie O'Hara?" asked Roberto.

"No, what's that?" asked Mary.

"Well now, some years ago, as the story goes. There was this local farmer called Willie O'Hara. Now Willie was a bit fond of a wee drop of the hard stuff. One weekend he was there, in the pub, and at the end of the night staggered to his car and got in. He managed to reverse it out a little bit, but was so full of whiskey he just stopped the car where it was, lay down on the seats and went fast asleep. When nearly all the customers were gone and the car park was almost empty, who turned up but a patrol of RUC."

"RUC?" asked Bob.

"The Royal Ulster Constabulary, the police."

"Ok, understand."

"Now the first thing they saw was this car, sittin' in the middle of the car park. 'Ah,' thought this sergeant, 'a drunk in charge of a car'. So they pulled up beside the car and the sergeant knocked on the window. There was no response from the snorin' Willie. Just then the head barman arrived with a customer. 'Is there a problem here?' says he to the sergeant. 'Well, I am afraid we will have to arrest this man for being in charge of a motor vehicle while under the influence of drink.' 'Is that a fact,' says the barman, looking around the car. 'John,' says he to the customer that was with him, 'Will ya go out the back shed and get me a saw so we can help the police here.' 'You want a saw?' asked the sergeant. 'Of course I do. There's no other way around it.'

The police man looked puzzled. 'I'm sorry, I don't understand', says he. 'Well sure, it's easy ta understand. De ya see that yellow line there, under the car? That side of it is Northern Ireland, and this side of it is the Republic of Ireland. Now, I would not want ya ta be breaking the law sergeant, bein' a good upstandin' citizen that I am. So, I am goin' ta help ya out. I will saw him in half, just above the waist there. You can arrest the half that is in Northern Ireland, and I will take the other half home, ta his wife. Being a good citizen, as I am, sure I would not want ya ta be getting into trouble arrestin' a man, or any part of him that was in another country. Sure, the ramifications would be a holy disaster.' The police sergeant just looked at the barman, said nothing, got into his car and drove off."

Everyone in the car was laughing, loudly. They all still had their glasses of drink, which Po explained, was an Irish tradition and had to be taken from the pub with them. Red held up his glass for a toast. They all clinked glasses.

"Bob, Mary, welcome to Ireland."

End

The Driving Test

1964

Red , Po and Anto were sitting in the first snug in Uncle Luigi's, chatting about Po's Driving Test that afternoon.

"The only thing I'm nervous about is the 'Emergency Stop'," said Po.

"That's the easiest part of the whole test, for God's sake. All ya have ta do is stop. What's hard about that?" commented Red.

"I know, I know. I am just nervous about it."

"Are ya not used ta stoppin', then?" grinned Anto.

"Don't you start," snapped Po.

"Jasus, I only asked a small intelligent question and his feet are hangin' outta my mouth."

"I know ya, Falsoni. You're as bad as him," said Po, nodding at Red.

"Now what did I do?"

"I know you two far too well. Yis'll try and wind me up about this stupid test, so ya will."

Anto and Red looked at each other.

"A don't know about you, Anto, but I'm cut ta the bone, so a am."

"Cut ta the bone? I'm just devastated."

"That's a good word, that. Wish I had thought of it."

"All ya had ta do was ask."

"Will, next time."

"Will you two stop? I'm nervous enough without yous winding me up. The least ya could do is give me a few tips," complained Po.

"He's right, Red. Give him a few tips."

"Ok, lets see . . . well now, I have found that the best way ta start gropin' a woman is ta start from the side and slowly slide your hand round ta the front. If ya go straight ta the front she'll push ya away. The other way it seems almost accidental, ya see, and she'll go with that."

"You're a real smart whore, Morgan, so ya are."

"It's just common sense, if ya think about it, Po."

"He's right, Po. Ya have ta be subtle. Ya can't be like a cow at a gate, ya know."

"If yous two aren't gonna help, then I'm goin'," said Po.

"Look, Po, your man will say to ya. 'I want ya ta do an Emergency Stop when a slap my hand on the dashboard'. Ya just hit the brakes," said Anto.

"Easy ta say," commented Po.

"Po, just try and stick his head in the windscreen," laughed Red.

"No, don't listen ta him, Po. Willie Johnston failed doin' that. He braked too hard and his back wheels skidded a few inches and he failed."

"A thought yis said it was simple?"

"Well, simple-ish," mused Red.

"Jasus, I should never have asked. I'm more nervous now, so a am."

"Po, ya'll just sail through, so ya will."

"Yeah, right, wishful thinkin'. What if he's an auld, cranky bastard?"

"Ah, well in that case, I have the answer. Just imagine him sittin' there with his trousers down around his ankles," smiled Red.

"Now, don't be stupid, Red. If he was ta do that, sure Po would only get all worked up."

"You're right, Anto. Never thought of that."

"Ta hell with you two. I'm goin' ta give my head some peace," said Po, as he stood up and left the snug.

"Now, there's thanks for ya," said Anto, seriously.

"No thanks in these wee, small people at all, ya know."

"None a'tall."

Po's test was set for three o'clock. At five, Po arrived at Red's house.

"Well?"

"Well, what?"

"The test?"

"What about it?"

"Jasus, did ya pass?"

"Long friggin' story."

"A thought it might be."

"De ya wanna hear, or not?"

"Tell me, tell me. A can't friggin' wait," laughed Red.

"Well, the guy that was testin' me must have been about 90, at least."

"He failed ya?"

"He took me all around the town, so he did."

"And?"

"At least I got the Emergency Stop right."

"Well done, and . . . ?"

"I was embarrassed at the traffic lights at the Savoy Cinema, so a was."

"What happened?"

"I was sittin' there, waitin' for the lights ta change, when my window was knocked."

"Your window was knocked?"

"Frig me, I didn't know where ta look."

"Who knocked your window?"

"Ya know your auld one, Maggie Turley?"

"Yeah."

"Was her. I opened the window and she started. She can't stop talkin', that one."

"What did she want?"

"She wanted me ta tell ma mom that the Kelly butchers were sellin' lamb chops at half price."

"Holy shit! An' in the middle of your test," laughed Red.

"Then, the lights changed. I told her I had ta go."

"And . . . ?"

"She wanted ta tell me about her son breakin' his arm. I know the wee bastard. Pity it wasn't his neck."

"Did your man say anything?"

"Just at that moment he says, 'Madam, we are in the middle of a Driving Test.'."

"What did she say?"

"Well, before she could say anythin' the cars behind me started blowin' their horns."

"Not surprised."

"I just said, 'sorry Mrs. Turley, I have ta go', and I drove off."

"Jasus," laughed Red.

"Anyway, he took me out the Rathfriland Road and a had to reverse and park."

"Did ya do it ok?"

"Would ya believe, I did it perfect."

"Well done. So ya passed?"

"After that, he told me ta drive back to the Test Centre."

"So, the test was over, then?"

"Yeah. He said that a had a few faults with stayin' the right distance behind other cars, so he did."

"He failed ya?"

"And said I'd have ta work on usin' ma mirror more."

"He failed ya, then?"

"Will ya wait, will ya?"

"I've been waitin' this half hour, for Christ's sake."

"Well, after all that, he handed me the list of all the things I did wrong."

"Po?"

"What?"

"Did ya pass the whorein' test, or not?"

"Sure, isn't that what I'm tellin' ya. Jasus, you're terribly impatient. Yes, I passed the test."

"At last."

"What, at last?" asked Po.

"And ya have the nerve ta tell me Maggie Turley talks a lot."

"Well I thought ya would want all the details."

"You're very kind ta think of me, Po. Ya know what? If ya had started talkin' ta your man that tested ya, he would have passed ya in five minutes, just ta get rid of ya."

"I was only tellin' ya what happened, for God's sake."

"Well, I'm delighted ya passed, anyway. Well done."

"And listen ta this, smart arse. At the end of the test he says, 'I was pleased that you didn't talk all the time and concentrated on what you were doin'.

Too many drivers talk far too much, and do not pay attention to their drivin'."

"Oh, my God, he's off again. Ya know, there should be a law against talkers like you for causing brain damage ta people."

"Is that so, fartface. Well let me tell ya this . . . . ."

End

The Dare

1965

"Well she looks pretty good outside," said Red, as he walked around Jumpy's new car.

"What's the engine like?" asked Anto.

"Running well. I had our Tommy, the mechanic, to check it out."

"Well, I wish ya all the best with her, Jumpy," said Red, seriously.

"Fifty pounds well spent, I think," smiled Jumpy.

"Well, on the face of it, Jumpy, looks like ya got a bargain," commented Po.

"So, tonight you'll have ta buy us a drink ta celebrate your new car," said Anto.

"Hang on, isn't it the other way around? You're suppose ta buy me a drink?"

"Jasus, no Jumpy," put in Po. "That's an English tradition, for God's sake. The ancient Irish tradition is, when ya get a new car, ya buy your friends a drink, so ya do."

"De ya think I'm stupid altogether, do ya? There were no cars in ancient Ireland, so how could it be an ancient Irish Tradition?"

Po looked at Red and shook his head.

"Sad, isn't it?"

"Just thinkin' the same thing ma own self," said Red, seriously.

"It's not the car, ya dope. It's the wheels, the transport. In ancient Ireland ya bought your friends a drink if ya got a new cart or a wagon or such like, ya see."

"Ah, right, got ya. Ok, I'll buy yis a drink tonight then, in the Waldorf, ok?"

"Sounds good ta me," smiled Anto.

When Jumpy left, Red looked at Po.

"Jasus, you're a sly wee whore. That was fast thinkin' about the wagon and stuff."

"A have ta admit it, me own self. It was good," laughed Anto.

"Well, when ya have a brain like me, and are talented like me, and of course, with my good looks, it's no big deal," said Po, seriously.

"I'm gonna punch him now, hard," said Red to Anto.

"No you're not, I want ta do it."

"Ok, toss for it, heads you get him, tails I do."

"Deal."

Red tossed a coin.

"Shit, it's heads. You get ta hit him . . . hi, where did he go?"

Later that night they all met up in the Waldorf bar, and true to his word, Jumpy bought a round of drinks. The group was made up of Anto, Jumpy, Dunno, Po and Red.

"Yis are lucky it's pay day. I spent all ma savin's on the car."

"Slainte. Here's ta your new car. Keep her between the ditches," said Po, raising his glass.

"Slainte," repeated everyone.

"Well, fair play ta ya Jumpy. At least ya completed one of the two Irish traditions after gettin' a new car," said Po.

"There's another one?" asked Jumpy, seriously.

"Sure there is. Tell him Red."

"Naw, better comin' from you. You're the expert in these things, isn't he Anto?"

"Now that's for sure," agreed Anto.

"Ok, right. I'll use my vast array of knowledge of Irish traditions then, to explain ta ya. Let's see. Well, as far as I remember, after we get our drink, we all have to write down a dare for the new owner of the vehicle ta do. He has ta close his eyes and pick one. If he carries out the dare successfully, the Gods will bless him and he will have good luck with his new transport."

"I'm not afraid to take a dare, so I'm not."

"Well done, Jumpy, but there's another bit to the dare I haven't told ya."

"What's that?"

"Ya don't do it on your own. Ya have ta have your best friend ta do it with ya, ta help if needed, and ta improve your luck, ya see."

"Will ya do it with me, Dunno?" said Jumpy, to his mate.

"No problem a'tall."

"Ok, so what do we do, then?" asked Jumpy.

"Wait an' I'll get some paper at the bar."

Po returned and tore up some paper giving Red, Anto and himself a piece each.

"Yous don't get ta vote since yis are doin' the dare."

"Ok."

"Now, yourself and Dunno go ta the toilet so we can fill in our dares."

When they had gone, Po whispered.

"Now, write down, 'do a streak'."

"Jasus, this is gonna be good," laughed Anto.

When they had finished writing, and Po had collected the papers, he explained in whispered tones his plan to Red and Anto.

When Dunno and Jumpy returned they found Red and Anto with tears running down their faces, in sustained laughter.

"What?" asked Jumpy, sitting down slowly.

"Nothing, was just tellin' the lads a joke a heard. Now, I have the notes, here. I'll put them upside-down on the table. Ya have ta pick one, ok?"

"Right."

Po laid the three bits of paper in front of him.

"Now put your finger on one of them."

Jumpy slowly placed his hand above the paper.

"I pick . . . this one."

Po grabbed the other two pieces of paper quickly, and put them in his pocket.

"Ok, let's see what ya picked."

Po turned the paper over.

"Not the one I was hoping for, but it will have ta do."

He handed the paper ta Jumpy.

"Jasus, it says 'do a streak'."

"What does that mean?" asked Dunno.

"It means we have ta pick a place, and ya both have ta streak."

"No problem. I'm not afraid ta do that," declared Jumpy.

"Where will we have ta do it," asked Dunno. "Oh, and I have a question, can we wear masks, so we won't be recognised?"

"I think we can all live with that," said Po, looking at Red and Anto, who both nodded.

"Now as to where? I think in the town would be a bad idea, so let's say . . . let me see . . . got it. The Lake Inn, in Camlough, ok?"

Jumpy and Dunno exchanged glances, and both nodded.

"No problem."

"Right. Do it tonight ok?" continued Po.

"Ok, tonight it is, then."

"Right, we will all meet in the café beforehand, ok?"

"Deal."

They all lifted their glasses and clinked them.

"Here's to ya completing the dare and gettin' loads of good luck," said Po.

*　　*　　*

Red, Po and Anto met in the café before Dunno and Jumpy arrived.

"Now are we all straight on the plan?"

Through their laughing, Red and Po mumbled they knew what to do.

Dunno and Jumpy arrived, and sat in the snug beside Anto, Red and Po.

"Now, I've done this dare, my own self, so I will give ya some tips that will make it work like a charm, ok?" said Po.

"Ok," answered both, Jumpy and Dunno.

"Right. Now, I suggest ya pull in just outside the bar in a dark spot and get stripped. Get your masks, or whatever yis are wearing, on. Leave the engine runnin'. This is very important for gettin' a fast getaway," said Po.

"Sounds simple ta me," smiled Jumpy. "It'll be a good laugh, so it will."

The two daredevils left, watched by Red, Anto and Po who waved after them.

"Right, let's go," said Anto.

All three ran across the road to where Anto's car was parked. In a few moments they were on their way after Dunno and Jumpy.

"Don't get too close," said Red.

"With that car in front, they can't see us. Don't worry."

In about ten minutes they had reached the village of Camlough. Anto saw Jumpy's car indicate and he pulled in about two hundred yards away, where they could get a good view of what was happening. About five minutes later, they saw the doors of Jumpy's car open and two naked bodies get out. Both were wearing balaclavas. They ran toward the front door of the Lake Inn.

"Right. Now Anto, go, go."

Anto's back tyres skidded as he took off at speed. A few seconds later, he pulled up behind Jumpy's car. Red jumped out and got into the car which had the engine running. Anto raced off at speed, as did Red, close behind him. When they reached Newry, Anto pulled in near the Police Station in Edward Street. Red parked behind him, got out, and got into the back seat of Anto's car, which took off as soon as he closed the door.

"Did ya remember ta leave the keys in the car?" asked Po.

"Yeah, I did, left their clothes too," laughed Red.

Five minutes later they were all seated in Uncle Luigi's Café.

"Went like a friggin' charm," laughed Anto.

"That it did," giggled Po.

"Will we see them tonight, de ya think?" asked Red.

"Doubt it, some way or other," laughed Anto.

"What do ya think they'll do?" asked Po.

"Anto? Phone," came the booming voice of Uncle Luigi.

"Comin'. Wonder if that's them?" Anto asked his companions.

Five minutes later, he was back.

"It was them, come on. We have ta pick them up," laughed Anto.

On the way to the car Anto explained what he was told.

"They said they came out of the pub, leaving all the women squealing, and their car was gone," laughed Anto.

"What did they do?" asked Po.

"They took off, what do ya think? They kept to the dark side of the street and hid every time a car passed, until they got to a phone."

"Where did they get the money ta ring?" asked Red.

"They 'tapped' the number."

(Tapping the phone: An illegal way of using a public phone by tapping the number on the receiver like Morse Code.)

"Never thought a that. Where are we pickin' them up?"

"Just outside Camlough."

Anto slowed down as he approached the village and began flashing his lights, as instructed. Suddenly, from a lane, two naked bodies appeared, and ran to the car, getting into the back seat quickly.

"Jasus, Anto, frig me, thanks for comin'," said Jumpy, breathlessly.

"No problem. Now tell us what happened?"

"Well, we stripped and ran into the pub. There was a friggin' party, or somethin' on. The whorein' place was full. Loads of dirty bitches there in Camlough, so they are."

"Why's that?" asked Red.

"They were tryin' ta grab ma willie, so they were," said Jumpy.

"They were grabbin' my bum, so they were," added Dunno.

"Was your wee willie too small ta grab, Dunno?" asked Po.

"Frig off, ya fruit," was his reply.

"Anyway, when we got outta the pub some bastard had stole ma car."

"Jasus, Jumpy, that's a holy terror. Stole your friggin' car, the bastards did?" said Red.

"Friggin' did. I'll have ta go ta the police won't I?"

"Ya will, Jumpy, but if I were yourself, I would put some clothes on, first," laughed Anto.

Po nudged Anto, directing him to turn down Edward Street. He did so, and they were soon approaching the spot where Jumpy's car had been left.

"Jasus Christ, look," shouted Po.

"What is it?" asked Red.

"Stop Anto, stop. Isn't that Jumpy's car over there?"

"Jasus, you're right. I think it is," said Anto, in a surprised voice.

"That's my car, all right. Let us out, Anto."

"Wow, hold on a minute there, Jumpy. What if someone see's ya gettin' outta my car in your birthday suit? I would get the name all over town as a fruit."

"There's nobody about Anto. Please?" said Dunno.

Anto pulled up and the two jumped out, racing to Jumpy's car. The window opened.

"The keys are still in it, and so are our clothes," shouted Jumpy, in a relieved voice.

"Ok, meet yis back at the café," shouted Anto, as he drove off.

By now Red and Po were in fits, laughing.

"Was that good or not?" asked Anto.

"It was whorein' brilliant," laughed Red. "Sure you're a wee miniature genius Po, so ya are."

Later in Uncle Luigi's, the three were sipping Cokes, when Jumpy and Dunno walked in.

"Jasus, ya saved our lives, so ya did, Anto," said Dunno, sitting down.

"Ah sure, it was what he was born ta do," said Po, patting Anto's head.

"And, we even got the car back," added Jumpy.

"We were lucky we weren't caught, weren't we," added Dunno.

"Not yet," said Po.

"What de ya mean, 'not yet'?" asked Jumpy.

"Well, I was thinkin'. Do ya remember one day we were out at the County River swimmin', an I asked ya what the mark on your arse was?"

"Yeah, ma mole."

"How many people were there, Jumpy?"

"Jasus, loads," laughed Jumpy.

"An, how many have a mole on their arse do ya think?"

"Just me, why?"

Po looked at Red.

"Bad, isn't it, Red?"

"Bad? Christ, I would say a disaster, so a would."

"What are yis talkin' about?" asked Jumpy.

Po looked up at the ceiling.

"I can see a couple a the boys talkin' outside Woollies tomorra'. 'Did ya hear about the two guys streaked in a pub in Camlough? They say one of them had a mole on his arse'."

"Holy Jasus," mumbled Jumpy.

" 'Wait a minute' one of them will say, 'sure, doesn't your man, Jumpy Jones, have a mole on his arse'?"

"Oh shit! I'm whorein' dead."

"Wait till a tell ya. Every fruit in the town will be after ya. Sure, ya'll be nothin' less than a celebrity, and if they know it was you, it won't be hard ta put it together that it was your own mate, Dunno here, that was with ya," added Anto.

"Jasus, Jasus. We're done for," mumbled Dunno.

"Well, not yet. But I would watch what part of the town I go ta, in future."

Red lifted his Coke bottle.

"A toast, then."

They all lifted their bottles and clinked them.

"Another old Irish saying . . . 'He who shows his willie to all in a pub, is inviting the fruits ta give it a rub'," said Red, seriously.

"Ah Jasus. That's it. I'm finished, ruined, destroyed, so I am," said Jumpy, holding his head.

"I was just thinkin'," said Anto, looking at the ceiling.

"If you guys are goin' ta continue comin' in here, Uncle Luigi will have to change the name of the café."

"Ta what?" asked Red, keeping a straight face.

"Uncle Luigi's Fruit Merchants Fish and Chip Emporium."

End

The Football Programmes

1965

"When will ya be back?" asked Red's mother, Jean.

"Monday," replied Red, as he zipped up his bag.

"I'm goin' ta clean this room out over the weekend. It looks like a bomb hit it."

"It's not that bad, Mom, just a little untidy."

"Untidy? I've seen cleaner rubbish dumps!"

"Ok, make it lovely and clean, then," laughed Red.

"I will, and it had better stay that way, I'm warnin' ya."

"I will take my shoes off at the door, from now on," Red smiled.

His reactions, honed through long experience, allowed him to move fast enough to miss his mom's hand.

Red was off, for the weekend, to Dublin. As well as staying with a friend he had met when he worked there last year, called John Deere, he was going to see the Republic of Ireland V Iceland at Dublin's Dalymount Park. John was a small, thin man, in his late twenties. He and Red hit it off the first time they met, and had become good friends. Red was delighted when John contacted him to let him know he would be working in the Newry factory for three months. When he had returned to Dublin, they always made sure to stay in touch.

*   *   *

"So, welcome back to Dublin," smiled John, when he met Red at Amiens Street Station.

"Sure if it isn't himself, how are ya John?" smiled Red.

"Good, got the tickets and all for the match tomorrow. That reminds me, I have this friend, Johnny Moran, who, like you, is a nutter for Football Programmes. He has hundreds of them. He's lookin' forward ta meetin' ya."

"Jasus, wish I had a known that, I could have brought a few of my programmes ta show him. We might have been on ta swap a few."

"Never worry, I'm sure yis will have plenty ta talk about," laughed John.

Later that night, John's friend, Johnny Moran, called to John's house to meet Red. He brought with him a large box of Football Programmes to show him. There were a lot Red already had, but a few he didn't, and Johnny was willing to swap. He mentioned at least five programmes he wanted and Red had them. It was agreed they would swap addresses and send each other the programmes.

They went to the International match and had a great time. Ireland won 4 – 2.

On Monday, Red arrived at Edward Street Station at lunchtime. He walked the two miles to his home on Castle Street and managed to resist the temptation to call into Uncle Luigi's Café, on the way. He was anxious to get rid of his case and get changed.

"The wanderer returns," smiled Granny Morgan, as Red entered the kitchen.

"Hi Granny."

"Did ya have a good time?"

"Great time."

"Ah, you're back. Thought I heard ya," said Red's mom, entering the kitchen.

"Hi Mom."

"Before ya get settled, come up to your bedroom with me."

"Right now?"

"Right now."

Red followed his mom up the stairs, carrying his case.

"Now, this room has been cleaned, and I want it to stay the way ya find it."

They entered Red's bedroom. Red put down his suitcase and looked around. He turned to leave.

"Where ya goin'?" Jean asked.

"Sorry, I think I'm in the wrong house."

He got punched on the arm.

"Now, I want ya to keep this room clean, right?"

"Wow, ya did some job here, Mom. It's like a new room, so it is."

Red walked around the room, looking in every corner.

"Ya did some job, Mom. Where's my programmes?"

"Your what?"

"My Football Programmes. They were in a cardboard box here, beside the wardrobe."

"I threw them all out. I looked at them and there were some over 20 years old. I dumped the lot this morning. They were just gatherin' dust."

Red didn't answer. He just stood and stared. The colour had left his face.

"Mom, please tell me you're jokin'?"

"Why, did ya want them?"

"They were irreplaceable. They were worth over £200."

"Yeah, I'm sure," laughed Jean.

"Where did ya throw them?"

"They went inta the bin lorry this mornin'."

"Oh, my God."

*   *   *

"Jasus, a would have died, or even worse, if it had been me," said Po, seriously.

"The day's not over, yet," mumbled Red, face in hands.

"Can't believe it. Even the European Cup programmes?" asked Anto.

"Even them. The FA Cup Finals and the Manchester United ones, too."

"Christ, now that's what I call a disaster, for sure."

*   *   *

Monday evening, Red was in his back garden, when he heard Po's voice.

"Hi, shitface."

"Hi, your own self."

"What's happening?"

"Nothin'."

"Ya seem a bit down."

"Wouldn't you be?"

"I suppose, but ya know what they say, every cloud has a silver linin'."

"In my case, it's lead."

"Are ya comin' down ta Anto's?"

"Naw, stayin' here. By the way, what happened ta you? You're covered in muck."

"Just doing a bit of work for a friend. Come on up ta the house and I'll let ya make me a cuppa."

Red made the tea, accompanied by two very large jam butties.

"By the way, Anto, Bishop, Topcoat, Jumpy and Dunno send their regards, and said they hope ya will be happy soon, and give them money, and fish and chips and Coke, and coffee and ice cream and sweets and . . ."

"Po, Po, stop! What the hell are ya talkin' about?"

"Didn't a tell ya? Jasus, my head goes on me, sometimes. Come with me a minute."

Po led Red to the hallway. He placed his foot on a cardboard box sitting in the corner.

"Now, ya see, all it took was a wee bit of brains ya see, my brains in fact, which, ta be honest, is a lot more than a wee bit of brains."

"Po, what are ya on about?"

"Meself and Anto was tellin' the boys about your misfortune regarding the programmes, ya see."

"Ok, and?"

"Well, sure didn't a brainwave hit me, right on top of the head."

"If ya don't tell me what you're talkin' about, it won't be the only thing ta hit ya on the top of the head."

"I thought, ya see, what would happen ta your programmes? They would be taken ta the dump on the Armagh Road, right? Well, from there it was simple. We all raced off ta the dump and told the guy there what lorry drop we were lookin' for and he showed us. It took hard work, sweat, blood and a few tears and loads of shit and muck, but finally we came up with this," said Po, indicating the cardboard box.

Red looked at Po, then at the box. He bent down and opened it.

"Oh my God! I don't believe it!"

"What do ya think?"

"I don't friggin' believe yis got ma programmes."

"We did. Sure, aren't we just great guys, altogether?"

"I don't believe it. I just don't believe it."

Red grabbed Po and hugged him. He was quickly pushed away.

"Now, just because a did ya a favour doesn't mean ya can take advantage of ma body, ya fairy."

"A don't know how ta thank ya, Po."

"Well, from now on ya can stop callin' me names, right?"

"Callin' ya names? Me? Listen, ya wee shitfaced whore, I hate it when ya tell lies about me, so a do."

End

The Club

1971

"Hi shithead, wait up."
Red turned to see his pal Po running to catch up.
"Well if it isn't fart face," smiled Red as Po arrived beside him.
"Thought you were still in Dublin?" commented Po.
"I was, just got back this morning, goin' back tomorra."
"How's it goin' there?"
"Jasus, don't ask."
"Bad, huh? So tell me then, are ya outta work too?" continued Po.
"No, not exactly, just that I got landed with a new job out of the blue last night and it has sort of knocked me for six."
"Wow, Jasus, must be some job."
"That it is, how you doin'?"
"I got paid off this week, no work for frig sake."
"Really? I thought that was a job for life?"
"So did I, but it must be in some other friggin' life."
"So what are ya goin' ta do?"
"Don't know, maybe go to England."
Red stopped suddenly and rubbed his chin.
"Jasus Christ, this could be a blessin' in disguise ya know."
"What?"

"Let me ask ya a question, would ya work in Dublin?"

"Ya mean, move ta Dublin?"

"Yeah."

"I might, why?"

"I have a job for ya."

"You're serious now, no messin'?"

"No messin', I have the perfect job for ya, perfect, ya'll love it, but it's only for eighteen months."

"Shit, I'll take it. At this stage I'd take it if it was only for a month."

"Let's go to Uncle Luigi's and ya can buy me a coffee and a fish and chip and I'll tell ya all about it."

"Some things never shitin' change do they?" said Po shaking his head.

Ten minutes later both were seated in the first snug in Uncle Luigi's Café tucking into their fish and chips.

"Christ I missed these fish and chips let me tell ya. Luigi's are the best in the world," said Red stuffing another forkful of chips in his mouth.

"Yeah, they're great, they're great, now tell me about the job will ya?"

"Well, last night I was out for dinner with a friend from Dublin called Joe Morley. Think I mentioned him to ya before."

"Right."

"Now, last week I gave my notice into the Freezer Company. I hated it."

"Yeah, last time I was talkin' to ya you were sayin' that."

"Anyway, I was tellin' the story ta Joe last night. Now Joe is a well off guy, he runs all sorts of businesses."

"Ok."

"Joe thought for a minute, and looked at me. He stands up and says, 'Be back in a minute'."

"He left?"

"Will ya wait? He went out of the restaurant and came back in a few minutes with a load of ledgers and a great bunch of keys. Well, he sits down with this great smile on his face and hands them ta me."

"What were they for?"

"That's the best bit. 'Here Red' says he, 'These are now yours'. "

"What were they for; you are the slowest whore in the world at tellin' a story, de ya know that?"

Red laughed and continued, "Well, ta make a long story short . . ."

"That'll be the day."

"Will ya shut your face will ya?"

"Well get on with it then."

"Says Joe, 'These are the keys of 'Capers' in Stephens Green'. "

"Capers, what's that?"

"It's a well known Nightclub."

"Friggin' hell."

"Says Joe, 'I used ta run it myself as ya know, but I just bought a new place in Malahide and I don't have the time now. It's closed till Monday to get some wiring done. The story is, I have sold it to an English crowd, who are goin' ta knock it down and build offices in eighteen months. Now, you can run it till then. All I want is one hundred pounds ta cover the rates every week and it's yours'."

"Jasus Christ."

"So will ya come?"

"What do ya want me ta do?"

"You'll be the Assistant Manager."

"Jasus, Assistant Manager. And I'll get paid an all?"

"How much were ya gettin'?"

"£63 a week take home."

"I'll give ya £75 a week, and free digs, are ya on?"

Po jumped up, leaned across the table, grabbed Red's face and planted a big kiss on his lips before he could pull away.

"Piss off ya queer," said Red in disgust rubbing his mouth.

*   *   *

Sunday morning Red and Po boarded the 10.30am train for Dublin at Newry's Edward Street Station. They had the carriage all to themselves.

"Have ya the kitchen sink in there?" said Red looking at Po's two cases.

"I have a lot of clothes ya know."

"Did ya bring your wee pyjamas with the wee rabbits on them?"

"Get stuffed ya bitch."

"Jasus, just askin'."

"What time do we get in to Dublin?" Po asked.

"We will be pulling in ta Amiens Street at 12.45pm."

"Right."

"Right."

"You're in one of your bloody smart moods today aren't ya, ya bastard?"

"Me?"

"You."

"I am sure I don't know what ya'r talkin' about," said Red innocently.

"Course not," Po snarled throwing a copy of the Frontier Sentinel Newspaper in Red's face.

Red laughed loudly.

"What's so funny?"

"Nothin', well yes there is somethin'. What will your position be in your new job?"

"Assistant Manager, why?"

"Now ya do know it's not a nine ta five job don't ya?"

"Yeah, so?"

"Well, ya will sort of always be on call, like on duty all the time, do ya understand that?"

"I can live with that, so?"

"Now what's your job again?"

"Assistant friggin' Manager."

"And my job?"

"Manager."

"Correct and right. Now, you will take your orders from me, no back chat, so sit down there, don't speak unless I ask you a question and get your feet off the seats."

"Mr. Manager?"

"Yes?"

"Would you do your Assistant Manager an enormous favour?"

"Of course young man."

"Go screw yourself."

"Charming, just charming. Terrible the language ya hear comin' from Assistant Managers these days, just terrible."

*   *   *

Red had a ground floor apartment on Elgin Road, in Dublin's Ballsbridge, near the American Embassy. It had two bedrooms, a bathroom and a kitchen, and was, by most standards, quite a desirable residence. Ballsbridge was quite a nice area of Dublin, Elgin Road was walled on both sides with trees and grass verges. Just around the corner from Red's apartment there was a large, well kept park. Five minutes along the road brought you to Dublin's beautiful Grand Canal.

Red was awakened by noises in the kitchen. He slowly got up, opened the bedroom curtains, and squinted as the morning sun met his eyes. He made his way slowly to the kitchen pulling on a wrinkled bathrobe as he went.

"The friggin' dead arose," greeted Po without looking around from the small cooker from which was emanating an aroma of bacon and eggs.

"Huh," was Red's reply as he slumped down on a chair at the small table by the window.

"A made breakfast because I am a nice guy, talented, and just well liked and loved."

"Do ya have to be so friggin' full of life in the mornin's? It's only 7.20am ya know?"

"The reason for that is because I am full of life in the mornin's."

Po slammed a plate on the table in front of Red. There were two fried eggs, bacon, fried soda bread and a tomato.

"I scraped the mould of the edge of the soda bread," said Po sitting down, carefully placing his own plate on the table with two large mugs of steaming tea, one of which he placed in front of Red.

"So what's the plan for today then?" asked Po putting some bacon into his mouth.

"Well, we'll go in this mornin' and have a good look around. The café staff comes in at eleven o'clock."

"How many staff are there altogether?"

"I was reading the wage ledgers last night. The day staff is one cook and an assistant cook, and two waitress's in the café, and two cleaners, who come in at 9am."

"What time do ya open to the public?"

"At twelve noon."

"For the lunch crowd?"

"Yeah. We stay open until 6pm. We close then until 9pm for the nightclub crowd."

"Then the night staff come in?"

"Yeah, there's two doormen, a cook, two café waitresses, two barmen, two bar waitresses and another doorman with that lot downstairs."

"I think we are goin' ta be busy bunnies," smiled Po.

"I'm beginnin' ta think so," answered Red seriously.

After breakfast, Red looked at the kitchen clock which read 8.15am. When he eventually managed with name calling and threats to get Po out of the bathroom, he had a quick shower and got dressed. When they were both seated in Red's Vauxhall Cresta, Po asked,

"Why did ya not take your car ta Newry?"

"Cheaper, and a lot quicker on the train."

"Ok, Jasus, there's a lot a traffic about."

"Wait till we get near Stephens Green."

When they did get there some 15 minutes later, the morning rush hour was in full swing. Red was lucky enough to find a parking place near the top of Grafton Street, just about 200 yards from the club.

"Is it like this every mornin'?" asked Po looking around.

"Well, I would think so, I'm never here at this time of the mornin'."

"Holy shit."

When they reached the nightclub, they stopped and looked up at the building. It was a Georgian House, with four floors above street level and one below. Above the door there was a neon sign reading, 'Capers Nightclub'. At the left side of the door was a small sign reading, 'Bammer's Café' and a menu underneath.

"Jasus, it's a lot bigger than I thought it would be," commented Po.

"Me too. It's a fine building though."

"That it is."

Red handed Po the ledgers, and fumbled with the keys until he found the right one. He opened the door and they entered into a large hallway with thick plush red carpet and red velvet, embossed wallpaper. An enormous glass chandelier commanded the centre of the hall.

"Christ, this is posh for sure," said Po in a hushed voice looking around.

Red didn't answer, he opened a large door to his left and entered the Bammer's Café. It was well laid out with twelve tables already set out for lunch with tablecloths and even a vase with flowers on each one. The cooking area was at the back of the room with just a counter leaving it open to the customers view. It was a bright room with cream flowered expensive wallpaper and a dark fawn carpet.

"Wow," exclaimed Po looking around.

"This place is really top notch isn't it?" said Red.

"Never seen anythin' like it," answered Po still speaking in a hushed voice.

"Let's have a look at the nightclub," said Red leaving the room.

They went through another large door and down some stairs and walked into the club. The room was in darkness.

"See if ya can find any light switches?" asked Red.

"Where would they be?"

"No idea, they wouldn't be here in the public area, I think they would be behind the bar."

Po lit a match and made his way toward the bar. Four matches later the room burst into coloured red and blue lighting.

"Holy shit," exclaimed Red looking around.

Po had returned and joined Red in his moment of awe.

"It's, it's friggin' beautiful," said Red in a low voice.

"It is, what a place."

The basement nightclub was designed as if it were a wine cellar, with stone archways, and barrels built into the walls. The lighting was subdued but very effective.

Suddenly a door closed upstairs and there was the sound of voices.

"Who's that?" asked Po startled.

"Most likely the cleaners, let's go an' meet them," said Red heading for the stairs.

At the top of the stairs they met two shocked cleaning ladies.

"Who are you?" asked one.

"I'm the new Manager, Morgan's my name, most people call me Red. This is the Assistant Manager, Hillen, most people call him Po . . . and don't ask," smiled Red.

"Oh thank God," said the second lady making the sign of the cross, "thought you were burglars or somethin'."

"Nice ta meet you Mr. Morgan. Mr. Morley rang me last night and told me ta expect ya taday. I'm Maggie, and this is Mary."

Maggie was a slightly overweight, blond lady, in her 50s, who, one would guess, was quite a good looking girl in her younger years. She still had a twinkle in her bright blue eyes. Her partner Mary was perhaps a little older and had a much harder life etched on her face. After some hand shaking and hellos, the ladies got on with their jobs and Red and Po ventured upstairs. On the first floor was the Manager's office and a large room filled with gaming machines. On the second floor was the card room. At the weekend Joe had told Red, some Italian, Chinese and local business men played poker here. The house got 20% of the pots and in return supplied drinks and sandwiches. Joe warned Red that at times these games went on all night. The top floor was not used so Red assigned it to Po as his office.

After the tour and an inspection of the books and staff information, Red sat back and looked across at Po who was engrossed in the drink and food requirements.

"Well, what's the verdict?" asked Red.

"It's a bloody big business, that I can tell ya."

"I was thinking of not openin' the Nightclub until Wednesday, we can use those couple of days to settle in, what de ya think?"

"I think that's one of your better ideas, which is easy ta remember since there aren't that many. It will give us a chance to get acquainted with the whole layout."

"We have the problem of the drink to look at."

"The drink?"

"Joe did not renew the licence since the place was closing and it is quite expensive."

"So, are ya still gonna sell drink?"

"Well, all they ever had was a wine licence anyways, and yeah, I am gonna keep sellin' drink. We will just have to work out a plan in case the cops come in."

"Ok."

"And since you have always been the planner, I will leave that to your good wee self."

"Gee, thanks."

"Don't mention it."

"Just did, are ya deaf? Won't people be coming to the door lookin' ta get in every night?"

"Was thinkin' about that. I am goin' ta put a notice on the door saying we are booked for private parties until Wednesday."

"Jasus, now that goes and proves everyone wrong."

"What?"

"Ya can think after all."

"Assistant Managers have been murdered in the past ya know."

"Maybe, but not the good lookin' ones," smiled Po as he posed.

"Want some advice?"

"What?"

"Get a bodyguard."

Red rang Joe Morley and told him of his plans. Joe thought it was a sensible idea. He told Red he was sending a friend around that afternoon called Paddy Whelan. He was a good man to know if you needed any tradesmen or workers.

The café staff began arriving at 11am and Red and Po introduced themselves to everyone. By 12.15pm, the café was full, with people waiting in a queue for seats. It appeared this was a popular spot in St. Stephens Green for lunch and after Red tasted the food he knew why. It was of excellent standard, at a good price and served quickly and efficiently.

Red and Po met in the hallway.

"Everything goin' ok in there?" asked Red.

"Seems ta be going well. I didn't interfere and just let them get on with what they usually do."

"Good idea. Any thought's on the drink problem yet?"

"A few, nothing very definite, goin' down there later ta have a closer look."

That afternoon, Red was in his office preparing a sign to put outside to inform customers about the nightclub closing for two days, when Po burst in.

"Got it . . . a whorein' friggin' shitin' brainwave so it is."

"What?"

Po was already around the desk and had Red by the arm.

"Come on, ya have ta see this so ya do."

Red was practically dragged downstairs to the Nightclub. Po took him behind the bar.

"Now, firstly, what's missin'?"

Red looked around the bar.

"What? Looks ok ta me."

"Ya remember I worked behind the bar in 'The Cellars' in Newry?"

"Yeah."

"Well, I am assumin' the law here is much the same as there, so, there's no friggin' wash hand basin."

"So?"

"Ah, this is where the idea began, have a look at this."

Po dragged Red out of the bar and into the small hallway at the side of the stairs.

"Look, what do ya see?"

Red inspected what Po was pointing at.

"Looks like an old door that was bricked up years ago."

"Correct and right. Now I went out the back and found a window. There is a wee small room behind the bar about 12 feet long and about 6 feet wide."

"Ok, and this is good because . . . ?"

Red was dragged back into the bar.

"Now listen carefully, right? We put a small sink just here for hand washing, right?" said Po pointing to a position on the back wall at the end of the bar.

"Now, ya will note, we are out of sight of the customers, right?"

"Ok," said Red looking puzzled.

"In the wee room behind here, we put two large, say, 20 gallon tanks on the wall. Do ya get it?"

"No, don't see where you're goin' with this."

"Now, we feed the tanks into the taps in the sink . . . get the idea?"

"Jasus, I think a know where ya'r goin' . . . we put wine in the tanks, and feed them ta the sink."

"Ya got it, red wine to the red tap and white wine ta the blue tap."

"Jasus Christ Po, a have ta tell ya, that's totally ingenious so it is."

"It'll work, I know it. They would never find it."

"I agree, brilliant, brilliant. Ok, let's get it organised right away."

∗　　∗　　∗

"Pleased to meet ya, Paddy," said Red, shaking hands with Paddy Whelan, a small, swarthy man in his 50's, with black, curly hair.

"Joe asked me ta call over and see if there was anythin' I could help ya with?"

"That's very nice of ya, Paddy, but ya should never ask me can ya help, a dangerous question," laughed Red.

Just then, Po walked into the office, and after the introductions were over Po asked, "That wouldn't be your Rolls outside, by any chance?"

"Yep, it's mine, all right. I have a few of them, and a couple of Bentleys. I run a Luxury Car Hire place."

"Beautiful cars," commented Po.

"They keep me busy," laughed Paddy.

"An idea just crossed my mind," said Po, rubbing his chin.

Red looked at Paddy.

"Was a short journey."

"Shut your smart mouth, bastard face. Paddy, would you by any chance have cars not out on hire at the moment?"

"The one outside, and a couple more. Why?"

"What would be the chance of ya parkin' them outside for a few hours?"

"Parkin' them outside. I suppose so, but why?"

Po turned to Red. "Remember we were goin' ta close tonight and tomorrow night and tell people we were havin' private parties?"

"Yeah, so?"

"How 'bout we have Paddy's cars parked outside and have the doormen workin'. We have loud party music and sounds comin' from the club, right?"

"Why?"

"Ya'll have ta excuse him Paddy, he's a bit slow, ya see. Look, everyone that comes ta the door is told we are totally full. Get all the staff ta park outside and with Paddy's cars the word will go round like wildfire that this is the 'in' place ta be, especially for the rich and famous. Get it Rolls, Bentleys parked outside?"

"A have ta say, Red, that's one hell of an idea, and it just might work," laughed Paddy.

"It is a hell of an idea. Let's do it, if it's ok with your own self Paddy?"

"No problem. I will have the cars here at about 8.30pm. If yous will give me a hand, I will take them back ta the garage at about 2am."

"Great stuff," smiled Red. "I'm glad a thought of this idea."

This only got him a severe punch on the arm, and a threatened punch to the chin from Po.

Everything went well that night; the doormen turned everyone away due to there being a full house. The luxury cars were also well-noticed by both pedestrians and passing traffic.

Po spent the night with Red, installing the two tanks in the little room behind the bar and fitting the new hand basin. By 1.30am, the job was finished and ready to go. Red put a few bottles of wine in the tanks to try everything out. Both the white and the red wine taps worked perfectly. They tried the taps quite a few times just to be sure.

Wednesday night came and everything was working well. Paddy got an electrician to fit an emergency warning light behind the bar. If the doorman pressed the 'Panic Button', a red light began flashing and they knew they were about to have a visit from the police. They did some dry runs with the staff before opening. The doorman pressed the emergency warning light, the staff immediately collected wine glasses from the tables and emptied them into the sink. The barmen got them into soapy water right away and began washing and drying. Trays of pre-filled glasses of orange juice were distributed to the tables. The whole operation took four minutes. The doormen had figured a way to slow the police down, if they did come. They would take a few minutes to open the main door. A second door, in the hall, was locked, and the second doorman took a few minutes to open that one. By the time the police would have reached to the Nightclub, seven minutes would have passed.

The night was a great success, as was Thursday, Friday, and Saturday. On Sunday night, the expected happened. The doorman noticed a police car stopping outside, at about 1.30am. He pushed the 'Panic Button' and the staff went into action. It took the police eight minutes to reach the Nightclub. All the customers were having a great time dancing and having their orange juices. Red approached the Sergeant.
"Hello, is there a problem?"
"And you are?"
"John Morgan, Manager," answered Red, extending his hand.
"Well we are just checking the place out. There is no Wine Licence here now, and we wanted to ensure the law was not being broken."
"No Sir, we no longer sell wine. Just soft drinks, as you can see."
"Do you mind if we check the bar?"
"Not at all. We have nothin' to hide."
Two police went around behind the bar checking underneath, as well as the shelving. They shook their heads at the Sergeant and left.
"Well, thank you. Keep running a clean place here, and you'll have no trouble from us."
"Wouldn't have it any other way, Sergeant," smiled Red.
They left. Everyone in the club was presented with a fresh glass of wine.

*   *   *

Two days later, Joe Morley called in to chat with Red.

"How's it goin', Red?"

"Great."

"And, I hear ya have the wine flowing every night."

"Too right, we have. Sure, we're washing our hands in it," laughed Red.

For the next 18 months, Red and Po ran the club very successfully, increasing the profits by over 30%. They had many visits from the police, and many thanks from them for running a 'clean house'.

One night, a few weeks after the re-opening Red and Po were having a quiet drink, after the club had closed, and everyone had gone. Red raised his glass in a toast, "To the Gods."

"To the Gods?" asked Po.

"Next ta J.C. his own self, who supplied the drink at that weddin' in the Bible, we are the only ones since then that have successfully turned water into wine."

End

Dandelion Market

1972

"Jasus, this is some place," remarked Po, as he stood looking around the Saturday indoor market on Dublin's Stephens Green. The market was called 'The Dandelion' and was, perhaps, Dublin's biggest indoor market.

"Didn't I tell ya it was a fantastic place?" replied Red.

"They sell everything here," added Po.

"A market like this must make a fortune," said Red.

"There's a thought," mused Po.

"What is?"

"Just wonderin'. Ya know, we could have a stall here, ya know."

"Sellin' what?"

"Knick knacks. Ya know, radios, tapes, soft toys. Anything and everything."

"Where would we get the gear?"

"I know a market wholesaler in Newry. Things in the North are less than half the price they are here, ya know. I would bet no one ever checks the markets."

"It's an idea, all right. Let's look into it."

They did look into it and decided to go with Po's plan. They bought enough items from the Newry wholesaler to get started. They got radios of various prices and sizes, marble ash tray sets, soft toys, household ornaments, kitchen ware and much more. They booked a stall and began their first venture into the markets.

At 8am that Saturday morning, Red and Po had their stall all laid out and ready for business.

"Well, what de ya think?" asked Po.

"I think it looks well. We have plenty of stuff."

"I messed up on them Bamvino transistor friggin' radios. Shit, we'll never get rid of all them. I only wanted 6 of them and ended up with 24. Don't know how it happened."

"Never worry, we'll get rid of them."

Po decided to place the two types of radios at the back of the stall, raised up on a cardboard box covered with red satin. He placed the box on its side to get more height, then went to the front with Red to look at the display just in time to see the box topple backwards and the two radios fall to the concrete ground. Both were smashed open.

"Shit, shit, and shit again," shouted Po, as he began lifting the two radios.

"You're havin' a bad wee day, crater. Sit down and rest your wee, poor self."

"Jasus, well what do ya know?" came Po's voice from behind the stall. He was on his knees, inspecting the broken radios, when Red arrived.

"What is it, now?" asked Red.

"I'm only a friggin' genius, that all," smiled Po.

"This radio, the Sanio, we have six of them. I'll see if I can get the dealer ta take five back."

"Why?"

"Why? Look at this?" said Po, showing Red the back of the Bamvino radio.

"What about it?"

"Look, can't ya see?"

"See what, for God's sake?"

"Ok, now, this is the Bamvino with the back off, right?"

"Right."

"This is the Sanio with the back off."

"Ok, so?"

"Can ya see the difference?"

"They look the same ta me."

"That's because they are the same. Look close. They're the same inside, exactly. But they have different casings."

"Yeah, I see that, a think. What's your point?"

Po had a broad grin on his face. He held a radio in each hand.

"Now ladies and gentlemen, step up please. Come closer and see for yourselves the bargain of a lifetime. In my right hand I have a radio from a well-known and respected company, Sanio. I will sell you this radio at well-below shop prices for £15.99. In my left hand I have a radio, exactly the same in every detail, just a different shell and made by Bamvino. Now this radio sounds the same, in fact is the same, except for two small differences. One, not a well known company and two, are yis ready for this? I will sell you this radio for £7.99."

"Jasus H. Christ," said a shocked Red.

"What do ya think?" smiled Po.

"Unbelievable. Totally un-friggin'-believable."

"Now, I'm happy I got 24 of these wee beauties. Sorry I didn't get a 100."

Po set up a special display with a new sign, making the two radios the main attraction. Within three hours all the radios were sold. At the end of the day, Red and Po went back to the club and had a glass of wine to celebrate.

"We will go ta Newry during the week and get a few cases of these wee goldmines," smiled Po.

"That we will. Sure, you're nothin' short of a wee genius, Po."

"I know, I know," said Po, leaning back in his seat and putting his feet up.

"Ya know, Red, it just goes ta prove ma philosophy on women."

"What are ya talkin' about now?"

"Well, sure ya know I'm a deep thinker, with great knowledge of women."

"Of course, a do Po, sure you're a legend in your own lifetime."

"I like you, Red, ya always tell the truth. Ya see, them radios are like women. On the outside they are all different, but, on the inside, they're all the same."

"Really? That's an interestin' point, I have ta say. I must pass on your deep thinkin' philosophical views to the love of your life when we go back ta Newry, this week."

"Ah Jasus, Red, don't be goin' and sayin' that ta herself."

"Well, now ya see, it's my own philosophy that, unlike radios, women may be, as ya say, all the same on the inside. But, there is one thing for sure, they don't all act the same. Now if I were ta tell your wee woman what ya said, she would batter ya from Hill Street ta Warrenpoint."

"All right, all right, point taken. Whore!"

End

Anything to Declare

1972

"Here we are. Do ya want tea or coffee?" Red asked Po.
"Well, since you're buyin', I'll have a milky coffee and an egg burger, thanks."
"Shithead."
"Asswipe. But, since you're buyin', you're a nice asswipe."

Red had pulled his car into a Petrol Station, just a half mile from the border with the Republic of Ireland. There were quite a few cars in the car park, that at first glance, one would assume had stopped for a snack or a coffee at the little diner and shop. This, however, was not the case. They were, in fact, waiting for the Customs Post to close for the night. Perhaps the only Customs in the world that would search your car for goods being smuggled into the South of Ireland at 11.15pm, then at 11.30pm, open the barrier, put the lights out, lock up, and go home. They did have a car on patrol at times, which would occasionally stop 1 in a 100 cars along the border to check them.

Red handed Po his burger and coffee through the window. When he got in Po said, "Thanks. Ya know a have ta tell ya, this is some car. I never was in a Jag before."

"She is a beauty, ok."

"And, in great condition. How much did ya get her for?"

"As a told ya, I got her from Joe Morley. He bought a brand new one. I got this for £500."

"Wow! That was some bargain, so it was."

"She is just under ten years old, though."

"I know, but there's not a scratch on her. Anyway, are ya goin' the main road ta Dublin?"

"Naw, think we'll go over the mountain and come out near the Ballymac Hotel."

"This is the one night we wouldn't need ta be stopped, for sure. The boot is packed full. We spent every penny we had."

"Correct and right. Look, there's the lights out now. We can leave in ten minutes."

"Can I drive?" asked Po.

"Snowball's chance in hell."

"Ah go on, a never drove a Jag."

"Last time I sat with ya, we were nearly killed."

"But I was only learning then, so a was."

"It was friggin' yesterday!"

"Spoil sport."

Red crossed the border past the now-empty and dark Customs Post. He turned left and headed toward the Cooley Mountain range. After travelling about five miles Red noticed a car's headlights in his mirror.

"We have company."

Po looked around.

"Shit, I hope it's not them bastardin' customs."

"It's them all right. They're flashin' me."

"Are ya goin' ta stop?"

"Are ya out a your wee head? Put your belt on. Let's see how good a driver he is."

Red floored the accelerator and the nose of the Jag lifted. In a few minutes he had lost the following car. As he was passing a forest on the left, he suddenly braked sharply and swung the Jag into a dirt road, switching off the lights when he was out of sight of the main road. He stopped the car.

"Come on, let's hide this stuff."

"Where are ya goin' ta put it?"

"In there, in the trees."

When all the goods from the boot had been hidden and covered with branches and bracken, Red drove the car slowly to the main road. There was no sign of any other traffic so he put on his lights and continued on his way.

"When will we go back for the stuff?"

"We'll go ta Dundalk, first. If we don't see the customs, I'll borrow John Mullan's car and we can go back and get the stuff. They know this car now."

"Sounds good. What if we do see them and they stop us?"

"Just follow my lead."

"Ok. Will do, oh fearless one."

Red laughed.

They were on the main road now, heading towards Dundalk.

"Look up ahead," said Red.

A Garda car and a Customs car had set up a road-block.

"Shit," muttered Po.

"Let me do the talkin'," said Red.

They stopped as directed by a Guard with a flash light. He waved them to the side of the road. When they had done so, the Guard and a Customs officer approached.

"Turn off your engine, Sir, and step out of the car, please," said the Guard.

Red did so.

"Are you carrying any goods liable for duty?"

"No."

"Will you open your boot, please?"

Red went to the rear of the car and opened the boot. The Guard shone his torch around and closed the boot.

"Is there anything inside the car, Sir?"

"Just my friend there, and he's duty free."

"I flashed you at the top of the mountain road and you accelerated off. Why did you not stop when requested to do so?" asked the Customs Officer.

Red looked around and pointed to one of the cars.

"Is that your car?"

"Yes."

Red walked to the car as if inspecting it. He walked around it and back to the Customs Officer.

"Perhaps it's just me, but does your car have a sign saying 'Customs' anywhere?"

"It is an unmarked Customs car, Sir."

"Unmarked is it. Hmm, I see. What time is it, Guard?"

The Guard looked at his watch.

"It's 12.30am, Sir."

"Guard, considerin' the troubles in the North, if you were comin' over a mountain road at 12.30 at night drivin' a Jag and an unmarked car came up behind ya and began flashing his lights for ya ta stop, would ya stop?"

"Well . . ."

"Too right, ya wouldn't. It could be a gang trying ta hijack your car, couldn't it?"

"I suppose . . ."

"Well, I didn't stop. And, in future, if any unmarked car tries ta stop me I'll do the same. Can ya blame me?"

The Guard looked at the Customs Officer, and then back at Red.

"Ok, Sir. Sorry for detaining you. Safe journey."

When he got clear of the road-block Po looked at Red.

"Ya were nothin' short of whorein' brilliant, Morgan. Wait till a tell Anto about this."

"Couldn't think of anythin' else, ta be honest."

"Ya did great. Whenever we stop, I'm goin' ta buy ya a penny chew."

"Jasus, you're way too friggin' generous."

"That's me, all right, well known for it."

They drove to Red's friend's house in Dundalk. He borrowed his friend's car and went back the way they came. The road-block was gone, as they had anticipated. They went back to the forest and retrieved their goods, continuing to Dundalk by a different route this time, and made it safely. The goods were swapped back to Red's car and they headed back towards Dublin. Customs never really went as far as Dundalk. They stayed within a couple of miles of the border.

"Well, wasn't that a bit of excitement, for sure," laughed Po.

"Excitement I could do without."

"Ah now Red, sure wasn't your wee heart just thumpin' with it all?"

"I am beginnin' ta think I am a genius, ya know."

"Why's that?"

"A didn't let ya drive."

"And . . . ?"

"We would have ended up in the forest all right, most likely on our roof, with a tree sticking through the windscreen."

"I'll have ya know I am a brilliant driver."

"Ya seem ta forget I've seen ya drive, ya dick."

"Ah now, hold on a minute, that wasn't my fault. It was that dog, so it was."

"Ah, yeah, the famous black dog."

"Well if it hadn't a been for the stupid dog, I wouldn't have hit the stupid ditch."

"Tell me this then, how come meself, Anto, Bishop and Ginger who were all looking at the road never saw any dog?"

"Not my fault yis are blind as bats."

"Right, Po."

"Right."

End

The Van

1972

It was just after 10am that Sunday morning at Red and Po's flat in Dublin, they were both sitting, having breakfast at the window table in the small kitchen.

"Is that Ollie Hogan just got out of that taxi?" asked Po, looking out the window.

"Jasus, it is," answered Red.

He got up and went to the front door, opening it just before Ollie arrived.

"And good morning ta your own self," smiled Red.

"Not a good morning. A very bad one," snarled Ollie.

"What happened?" asked Red, as Ollie passed him in the doorway, heading for the kitchen.

"Morning, Ollie," smiled Po.

"Hi Po."

"Well, tell us what happened?" asked Red, entering the kitchen behind Ollie.

Ollie took a seat at the table.

"Got up this mornin' ta go ta the market. When I went outside, the friggin' van was gone."

"Gone? Ya mean stolen?" asked Po.

"Some bastard took it during the night."

"Jasus, Ollie, that's a bit a bad luck, all right. Did ya report it ta the Guards?" asked Red.

"First thing. They said they would watch for it."

"Jasus, maybe it'll turn up. Have a cuppa," said Red.

"All ma whorein' market stuff was in it. Over £1000 worth."

Ollie had a stall in Dublin's Dandelion Market in St. Stephens Green, and travelled most days to markets around the country. He sold kitchen paper towels and toilet rolls.

"Holy shit! That is a big loss. Are ya insured?"

"No, just my luck. The insurance ran out last month, and a was a bit short."

Red poured Ollie some tea and sat down.

"What can we do ta help Ollie?"

"Well, I need ta use your phone. I haven't got one at my flat."

"Help yourself," said Po.

"Are ya lookin' ta borrow a van?"

"What for? I have nothin'. All ma stuff was in the van. That was ma wages for the next visit ta the wholesalers and ma wages for the month."

"Jasus," replied Red.

"I gave your phone number ta the Guards. Hope that was ok."

"Sure, no problem, Ollie," replied Red.

"I'll make a few calls. Any chance of a lift inta town?"

"No problem. Was goin' inta the club anyway, this mornin'."

Ollie Hogan was around 10 years older than Red and Po. He, too, was from Newry, but had been living in Dublin for many years. He had found out that Red had taken over Capers nightclub and became a regular customer.

Two weeks passed and there was no word from the Guards about the van, until one Saturday morning the phone rang about 8.30am.

"Hello, this is the Garda Síochána in Finglas. Can I speak to Mr. Hogan, please?"

"He's not here at the moment. Can I take a message?" asked Red.

"Would you be kind enough to tell him we have his van here, in our yard in Finglas. He would need to come here today, if possible, with his Driving Licence, the van keys, and proof of ownership."

"That's great news, Guard. Ollie will be delighted. Is there any damage ta the van?"

"Not that I could see, seems to be ok."

"I will have him there today for sure. Thanks."

Red and Po immediately drove to Ollie's flat in Rathmines. It took 10 minutes of knocking and shouting before Ollie answered the door.

"Not so loud, ma head's gonna burst."

"Ah, de ya have the wee hangover, de ya, Ollie?" mocked Po, laughing.

"Late night. Shush, will ya. De ya have ta breathe so loud?"

"Well I am the bearer of good news, Ollie. Got a call this mornin' from the Guard's at Finglas. They have your van and it's not damaged."

"Ah Jasus, that's friggin' great news. What do a have ta do?"

"Well, first and foremost, I think ya need ta put on some clothes, next get on the outside of a strong black coffee and we will take ya ta Finglas."

After listing all the documents Ollie would need, and the 30 minutes spent looking for them, and the 30 minutes for the shower and the coffee, they were on their way.

"Did the Guard say if ma gear was still in the van?" asked Ollie.

"Never thought ta ask, Ollie. Was just glad to get the news that the van was ok."

"Ok. A would say it was well cleaned out, by now," mumbled Ollie.

When they arrived at the Garda Station in Finglas they made their way into the reception area and approached the large counter. A tall ginger-haired Guard was writing in a ledger, leaning on the counter. He looked up.

"Morning. May a help you?"

"My name's Oliver Hogan. I understand ya got my van back that was stolen."

"Ah yes, Mr. Hogan. They found it last night in Cabra, and it was brought here. Did you bring all your documents?"

Ollie produced all the required documents and the Guard opened a drawer and placed a very large form on the counter.

"We have ta get this filled in, bureaucracy, I'm afraid," laughed the Guard.

Some 20 minutes later the form was completed, the documents were checked and duly noted and the Guard asked them to follow him out to the back of the station. On the way, he told Ollie that he was on duty when the van was brought in. There was no damage but it was totally empty.

When they got to the yard which was full of cars, some damaged and some wrecked, others looked like they were almost new, the Guard looked around.

"Someone must have moved it this morning. Stay here and I will go and check."

The Guard arrived back shortly, with a Sergeant by his side. They both looked around the yard.

"Mr. Hogan?" asked the Sergeant.

"That's me."

"I am afraid I am at a loss to tell you where your van is. We checked with everyone inside and it now appears, and I am very embarrassed ta say, it has been stolen again."

"Ya have got ta be friggin' kiddin' me?" replied Ollie, in a raised voice.

"I'm afraid not. I wish I were. If ya come back into the station we will need to fill in a form re the stolen van."

Ollie looked at Red.

"This has got ta be the friggin' stupidest thing I have ever heard. A stolen van, recovered by the Guard's and stolen again from their yard? I just don't believe it. It's like somethin' from a slapstick comedy."

"Ollie, I'm sorry," said Red, biting his lip. "I have been trying ta keep a straight face."

The forms for the stolen van were completed, and this took a lot more forms and a lot more time, because the van had now been stolen from Garda custody.

Ollie looked up at the Guard behind the counter.

"That's some name yis have, Guard. Yis guarded my van well, I have ta say."

"I can understand your feelings, Mr. Hogan."

"Tell ya what. I won't bother suin' yous, if ya do me a favour?"

"What is that Mr. Hogan?"

"If I bring ma ex-wife here, will ya guard her?"

End

The Drunken Driver

1972

As Red prepared to go home to his flat in Elgin Road, he was wishing he had taken Po's advice and gone home two hours earlier. He did, however, decide to stay on at the club, with a few of the customers, for a glass of wine, which turned into a few bottles of wine. It was now 4am, and Red was feeling a little the worse for wear as he got into his car, outside of Caper's Nightclub, in Dublin's Stephens Green.

He turned right, along the Green, passing the Shelborne Hotel, heading in the direction of Baggot Street. As he neared the canal, he saw a blue light flashing in his mirror. Immediately, he pulled in and stopped. A Garda Patrol car pulled in behind him, the driver got out and approached Red's car. He rolled down his window and said hello to the Guard.

"Evening Sir. Licence, please?"

Red produced his licence and the Guard inspected it under his flash light.

"Ah, Mr. Morgan, thought I knew the face. You're the Manager of Caper's Nightclub?"

"That's me."

"Could you step out of the car, please, Mr. Morgan?"

Red stepped out and closed the door.

"You have had a few drinks tonight, Mr. Morgan?"

"Just one or two glasses of wine after work, Guard."

"Hmm, one or two, huh?"

"That's it."

"Come with me, please, Mr. Morgan."

Red followed him to the Patrol Car. The Guard opened the front passenger door and nodded to the other Guard to get out.

"Take his car and follow me. Get in then, Mr. Morgan, please."

Red did as he was told. When the Guard got in, Red asked, "Are ya arrestin' me, Guard?"

"Where do ya live, Mr. Morgan?"

"Elgin Road, just facing the American Embassy."

The patrol car drove off, followed by Red's car.

"Are ya takin' me home, Guard?"

"That's what I'm doin'."

"Can I ask a question?"

"Sure."

"Why did ya stop me? I thought I was drivin' perfectly, like a wasn't speedin' or anythin'?"

"You're right. Ya were driving perfectly. That's why I stopped ya."

"I don't understand?"

"Well, ya see, I have been on the force for 22 years now. You are the very first driver I came up behind at 4'o'clock in the morning driving exactly at the speed limit, the correct distance from the footpath, and using hand signals."

Red didn't answer, he just nodded.

"Is this it?" asked the Guard, as he pulled up outside Red's flat.

"This is it."

"Now listen very carefully. Don't ever let me catch you driving again with drink in you, or you will regret the day you ever met me."

"I understand, and thanks very much, Guard."

The second Guard arrived and handed Red the keys of his car.

"Ya made it home, then," came Po's voice from the kitchen doorway.

"Just. Ya want some coffee?" asked Red.

"Naw. Goin' back ta bed. Was that a Garda car outside?"

"Yeah, they drove me home."

"Crap."

"They did."

"Ya were arrested. Ah shit. They got ya for drink drivin'?"

"No."

"No? So why did they take ya home, then?"

"Because they said I was a perfect driver."

"Aye, right. Of course, they did. I have Marilyn Monroe in bed with me. So, if ya don't mind, I'll go back and join her. Night."

"Ok, night."

Red sat down hard on the chair almost spilling his coffee.

'Jasus, when ya tell the truth, no one believes ya.'

Five minutes later, the perfect driver was fast asleep at the kitchen table.

End

Goodbye to Caples

1972

Red and Po were on their way to Caples for the last time that Monday night. The eighteen months had passed quickly and they had both loved working there. It was, in many ways, a sad day for them, tonight was the last gathering of the full staff and the last time Caples Club would be open. Tonight was a 'Goodbye to Caples' party for all the staff and a few selected customers.

"This is the last time we will take this drive ya know," said Po.
"That it is, I enjoyed every minute. If you had not been working there it would have been perfect."
This only got Red a punch on the arm.
"Typical, reverts to violence when his tiny brain can't cope."
Red laughed and ruffled Po's hair.
"You'll never change."
"Watch the hair will ya, it took me a half an hour to get it right."
"If ya took a lifetime ya'd never get it right."
"Better than your scruffy growth anyway."

They pulled up outside the club. There were quite a few cars there already. The club was of course closed to the public, last night they had a party for all the customers.

"Hi Red, ya made it then," smiled Joan, one of the bar waitresses who was standing talking in the hallway.

"Hi Joan, how's your own self? Good crowd here already it seems?"

"Yeah there is, most are down in the disco."

They both went downstairs to the now almost crowded disco. There were many hellos and handshakings, hugs and kisses. Tonight Red had ordered an 'open bar' for everyone. The café staff had also supplied sandwiches and snacks.

"Hi Red," said Sandra, one of the café staff as she took a seat beside Red at the bar.

"Hello Sandra, ya look beautiful tonight."

"Why, thank you very much. Are ya sad at the end of Caples?"

"I am indeed. Both Po and myself really enjoyed being here. It was a great eighteen months."

"On the subject of Po, I think some of the girls are planning something for him. As ya know, he was forever playin' tricks on them, so they thought this would be the last chance for them ta get their own back."

"What are they for doin'?" smiled Red.

"No idea, but I'll find out an let ya know later."

"Ok, Sandra, enjoy yourself."

Sandra reached over and kissed Red on the cheek.

"Thanks for being the worlds best boss," she smiled.

"Will ya stop, ya'll have me blushin' in a minute."

Near the end of the night, two of the girls approached Po.

"Come on Po."

"Where are we goin'?"

"We are goin' ta play a trick on Red."

"I'm all for that," laughed Po.

"We have ta bring ya up ta the café ta change."

"Change?"

"We need ya ta dress up as a cop. The girls have a uniform."

"I think I am goin' ta enjoy this," smiled Po.

*　　*　　*

"Red, come on quick," said Sandra as she grabbed Red's arm.

"What's up?"

"We are playin' that trick on Po but we need your help."

"No better man," laughed Red.

"Now, we got a policeman's uniform and we need ya to dress up in it, ok?"

"No problem, anything ta get one over on him," smiled Red.

"Ok, now go up to your office, I'll be there in a couple of minutes."

*   *   *

"Right Po, Kathy has gone to her car ta get the uniform. Quickly, strip down to your underpants, I won't look, promise."

Po giggled.

*   *   *

Sandra came into the office.

"Right Red, as fast as ya can, strip down ta your underpants, Kathy has gone ta get the uniform. I hope it fits ya."

"No problem."

Five minutes later a crowd of cheering people burst into the office. Red was grabbed unceremoniously and carried outside the front door of the club. He was brought to the railings surrounding the basement and tied to them; right beside his friend Po. Sandra hushed the crowd and said;

"Ladies and gentlemen. Over this past eighteen months, Red and Po were simply fantastic to work for. They were generous, understanding, caring, good fun and more than a little boisterous when it came to playing tricks on all of us."

"Here, here," shouted the gathering.

"The time has come, especially as it is almost Halloween, ta pay back some of those tricks. In America they have a tradition called 'Trick or Treat'. Here in Dublin we have changed it just a tad. Tonight it will be called, 'Treats for Tricks'. So, without further ado, for the many, many tricks played on us by Red and Po, we will, with pleasure, pay them back, with interest. These boxes contain loads and loads of treats, like, eggs, flour, tomatoes and kitchen leftovers. Please help yourselves and be generous in your giving."

"No, wait, wait, I have a bad heart, a bad liver and other stuff," shouted Po.

"Me too, I have Myxomatosis and a worse heart condition than him, and I have a bad knee and a bad shoulder, and ulcers and, and, and . . . ," shouted Red.

Before Red could finish, a rotten tomato caught him right in the face. When the boxes of treats were all used up, they decided that the two flour and slime covered figures had been very badly treated and they both should be washed down. Numerous buckets of water were tipped over them to clean them up. Cars passing now began to toot their horns in approval.

Red will always remember Sandra whispering in his ear before they were released from the railings; "Now ya see Red, yis think yis are a smart lot in the North don't ya? Well, not as smart as us Dublin gals. We got yis good, didn't we?" she laughed.

As the night came to an end, everyone left together. Red turned the key in the lock for the last time. Goodbyes were said to all with kisses, hugs, and even some tears. Red and Po waved goodbye and drove off into the Dublin night.

A couple of minutes later, Po turned to Red.

"When do ya think they will notice?"

Red looked at his watch.

"A would say about now. Not easy ta start cars with the plug leads disconnected."

"Not easy a'tall," smiled Po.

The two burst into laughter, another chapter in Red and Po's lives had come to an end.

End

Anto's Big Question

1972

Red and Anto were sitting in Uncle Luigi's Café having coffee. The mood, for lookers on, would have appeared serious.

"So what do ya think?"

"Jasus Anto, I don't know? A haven't been down that road yet."

"Well ya must have some information on the bloody situation at least."

"Yeah, don't do it."

"You're a great help you are."

"Look, there are only two ways ta go, buy or ask, one or the other."

"I know, ya said, but if I buy and she hates it, shit, that'll ruin everything."

"Then ask her."

"I don't like the thoughts of that a'tall."

"Jasus help me," said Red putting his face in his hands.

"Why do things have ta be so friggin' complicated?" pleaded Anto.

"It's you that's complicated ya silly bastard."

"I know, I know. Jasus."

"Here's the wee man, maybe he'll come up with somethin'."

Po arrived with a great smile across his face and sat down.

"Well, if it isn't Bill and Ben the Flowerpot Men."

"What are you all smiles about?"

"Just full of the joys of spring."

"Ah ha," said Red looking at Anto.

"Ya think?" asked Anto.

"Looks that way."

Anto bent over and peered into Po's face, squinting to see better.

"Yeah, I see what ya mean."

"What are yous two fruits on about?" laughed Po.

"Frig me Anto, it was well overdue anyway."

"It was, it was, well overdue."

"What?" asked Po raising his voice.

"Ya got it, didn't ya, ya wee rascal?" laughed Red.

"Got what?"

"Jasus I knew it, he got it Anto," smiled Red.

"Frig me he did, you're right."

"Are yous two shit heads goin' ta tell me what yis are talkin' about?"

"Last night, ya were out with Trish, weren't ya?" asked Red.

"So?"

"Where did ya go?" asked Anto.

"I told ya yesterday, we were baby sittin' in her sister's house."

"Ah ha," added Red.

"What's with the friggin' 'Ah, ha'?"

"Ya got it didn't ya?" said Red pointing his finger at Po.

"Got what?"

"Ya got inta her knickers, didn't ya, ya randy wee bugger," smiled Anto.

"Jasus Anto, my wee friend Po, he's only gone and lost his virginity," said Red seriously.

"Ya'll never get it back ya know Po," said Anto seriously.

"He's right, it's gone for good now," added Red.

"I didn't say I got anythin'."

"Po, look me in the eyes," said Red turning to face Po.

"Now tell the truth. Did ya do the job on lovely Trish?"

"I'm sayin' nothin'," said Po looking down.

"Jasus, would ya look Anto, he's only goin' red."

"I am not ya bastard."

"You're right, he looks like the tail light on a lorry, would ya look at the colour of him. Come over here till a warm my hands," laughed Anto holding his hands up to Po's face.

They were quickly brushed aside.

"Yous are makin' me blush so ya are."

"Look Po, seriously now, Anto there, and me own self, are your two bestest friends in the whole world. Sure ya can tell us the details, can't he Anto?"

"Of course he can, friends don't have secrets ya know. Did ya get her naked Po, did ya?"

"Anto, you're like a bull at a gate so ya are. Ya don't rush these things. Now Po, how did ya get the dress off, or did ya just pull it up?" said Red leaning his chin on his hands.

"I'm tellin' you two shit heads nothin'."

"Ya know Anto, I'm beginnin' ta get all choked up so a am," sobbed Red.

"There, there Red, it's all right," said Anto in a comforting voice as he patted Red's shoulder.

"But my wee friend, who I played football with, played marbles with, helped through difficult times like when he caught his wee willie in his zipper, he's only gone and become a man Anto."

"I know, I know. Hard ta believe isn't it?"

"Yous two are nutters so ya are."

"I hope ya wore the condom on your head like you're supposed ta on your first time Po?"

"Very important that Red," added Anto.

"Tis indeed."

"And I hope ya put her knickers in your pocket nice and tidy too?"

"What are ya talkin' about, knickers?"

"Anto, he doesn't know."

"Everybody knows for Christ's sake, Po, ya did take the knickers didn't ya?"

"No, don't be stupid," laughed Po.

"Ah Jasus Christ Po, please don't tell me ya just threw them ta one side?" said Anto.

"What? Ya mean ya just threw them on the floor?" added Red.

"A just put them on the sofa."

Red and Anto looked at each other and burst out laughing. They cheered and applauded, and shook hands.

"What, what for frig sake?" pleaded Po.

"Got ya Po," laughed Anto.

"What do ya mean?"

"We got ya to admit ya got her knickers off ya dope, which means ya got your wee willie where ya have been tryin' ta get it for a year," laughed Anto.

"Shit," said Po, putting his face in his hands.

This only made Red and Anto laugh all the harder.

When the conversation concerning the loss of Po's virginity, the details of which were expertly prised from Po, had ended, the subject returned to Anto's dilemma.

"So what are ya goin' ta do then?" asked Po.

"Don't know."

"Hold on a minute Anto, don't you Italians have traditions about these things?" asked Red.

"Come ta think about it, there are traditions, yeah."

"Well?"

"Not sure what they are exactly, I'd have ta ask Uncle Luigi."

"Does he know what ya intend ta do?"

"Yeah, told him yesterday."

"Well go and ask him then," said Red.

"Now?"

"Now."

Without another word, Anto left the snug and went into the kitchen. Ten minutes later he reappeared with a great grin across his face. He leaned across the table and kissed Red on the cheek.

"Get off ya friggin' fairy."

"I'm all set."

"What did he say?" asked Red rubbing his cheek with his sleeve.

"He went up the stairs and returned with this," said Anto opening a ring box.

"Holy shit!" exclaimed Po as he gazed on the beautiful diamond ring.

"Jasus, now that's a ring Anto," said Red taking the box.

"This ring was owned by my great, great, great grandmother or somethin'. It was handed down through the family. I had to promise that it would stay in the family and if I were ta have a son, he would get it."

"That solves all your problems in one go," smiled Po.

"No it doesn't, not all of them," said Anto.

"What else is there?" asked Red.

"She has ta say yes dummy."

"Ach, for God's sake, no problem there. Now ya will need ta put that ring away somewhere safe Anto should on the off chance ya might meet someone," said Po seriously.

"What the hell are you slabberin' about Hillen?"

"Well, ya know Sally a lot better than we do. She's one very smart lady. Do ya really think she's goin' ta take an ugly slob like you? Now, if she had the chance of gettin' me, well . . ."

This just earned Po a slap across the side of his head.

"When are ya intendin' to pop the question?" asked Red.

"Well, I hadn't thought of a time and date yet had I?"

"When are ya seein' her?"

"Tonight."

"Well then?"

"Ya think I should ask her tonight?"

"Why not?"

"Jasus."

"Well, what's the point of puttin' it off? Strike while the iron is hot."

"I will, Jasus, I will. I'll ask her tonight. I will."

"Good for your own self Anto," smiled Red patting him on the shoulder.

"Now, you two. Not a word to a soul about this, de ya hear me now?"

"Not a word," said Red, "promise."

"And you too shithead."

"Not a word, I promise too."

"Ok, I'm goin' ta do it."

Later that night, when the café had closed, Jumpy was keeping lookout at the front window.

"They're comin', they're comin'," he shouted.

A few moments later Sally and Anto walked in. Red was standing by the door. He knew by Anto's face that he was no longer in possession of his family's ring. He lifted Sally's left hand and smiled. Then turning around to the, what appeared to be, empty café he said, "Can we have a little respect here, there are engaged people in the house."

The café sprang to life with music and applause as bodies appeared from behind counters, under tables, in snugs and anywhere that afforded cover.

A table with candles had been prepared with a bottle of champagne chilling in ice. Uncle Luigi was standing at the table smiling. Anto and Sally were seated at the table and were being congratulated by everyone at the same time it seemed. All the gang were there to a man and a non smiling face would not have been found.

Later Anto cornered Red and Po.

"You two friggers promised you would not say a word ta anyone," said Anto pointing at Red.

"Well, Anto, it's like this ya see, my learned friend here advised me on the law. He will explain it to ya."

"It's like this . . ." explained Po.

"We both promised ya that we would not say a word to anyone, right? Now on further examination a discovered that if we were ta say more that one word, we would therefore not be breakin' the promise ya see."

"Two real smart arses aren't yis?" smiled Anto, as he hugged both.

"Well . . . ?" asked Red.

"Well what?" replied Anto.

"Details, details?"

"We went to the Imperial Hotel for dinner."

"Jasus, up market huh?" said Po to Red.

"Shut up you. It was a special occasion after all," said Anto.

"After dinner, I asked her if she would marry me and I produced the ring."

"And she didn't run out?" added Po.

"You'll get a dig in a minute Hillen. She smiled and said yes. I put the ring on her finger and that was that."

"Jasus, isn't that romantic Po."

"Can't speak, all choked up."

This got Po a punch on the arm from Anto.

"But a feel so sad," went on Po.

"Why is that wee Po?" asked Red.

"I really like Sally, she's a really nice girl so she is, how could she throw her life away like this?"

Just then, and just in time to save Po getting another punch, Sally arrived.

She hugged the two boys warmly.

"Thank yous so much for all this Red and Po. It was the perfect end to the perfect night."

"It was our pleasure Sally," said Red smiling.

"Now Anto, this will be the end of all your messin' around now. Ya'll have ta finish with that wee one in Hilltown and the other one in Dundalk."

Po was gone before Anto could get hold of him.

"I hope your undertaker is good at fixin' faces Hillen," he shouted after him.

End

The Engagement Party

1973

"So, I have something very important ta tell ya."

"It's ok Po, I know about your sex change," smiled Red.

"Will ya ever shut up and listen? This is serious."

"I'm listenin', I'm listenin'."

Red and Po were sitting in Uncle Luigi's Café sipping coffee that Saturday morning. The café was quite full with shoppers. Anto was working on the take-away counter and would occasionally stop to have a chat with the boys when work allowed.

"Well now, this is to be between you and me for the moment. I'll tell Anto later, but I don't want it gettin' out just yet, ok?"

"Sounds very serious," smiled Red.

Po reached into his pocket and produced a small square box. He opened it and inside Red could see a small solitaire diamond ring. He took the box from Po and looked at the ring closely.

"Is this what I think it is?"

"Yep."

"Jasus."

"What de ya think?"

"Must have cost ya a fortune."

"And then some."

"Well?"

"Well what?"

"When are ya askin' her?"

"Tonight."

"What if she suddenly comes to her senses and says no?"

"I think she'll say yes."

"Ya think?"

"I know."

"Ok, well, what can I say wee man. I hope she does say yes. I won't tell anyone until ya come back and tell me what she said."

"Promise?"

"I promise for Christ's sake. Hi, what age is Trish?"

"19."

"I have ta be honest Po, she is a catch."

"De ya think I don't know that? She's beautiful."

"Yep, she is. Could never figure out why she ended up with you though."

"Funny, ha ha," sneered Po making a face at Red.

*　　*　　*

Red was in bed reading a book he had borrowed from Anto called 'The Young Lions'. He heard a clatter on his window. He looked out and saw Po standing on the street below waving. Red waved back telling Po to wait. He got dressed, checking his watch while he did so to discover the time was 1.25am. On the way downstairs Red smiled. 'She must have said yes, otherwise he wouldn't be here ta tell me she turned him down.'

As he opened the door, Po brushed past him into the hall and continued to the kitchen. When Red arrived, he found Po putting the kettle on.

"Well?"

Po just smiled.

"She said yes?"

Po continued smiling. Red embraced him and the two danced around the kitchen.

"So, come on, I want all the details, did ya go down on one knee and all that?"

"No I didn't."

"Well, will ya friggin' tell me?"

"I brought her to the pictures, the Savoy, ta see Cleopatra with Richard Burton and Elizabeth Taylor."

"Jasus, I don't want the story of the friggin' movie."

"Will ya wait will ya? After the movie we went to the Florentine for a coffee, then we went for a walk along the canal. We were sittin' on the wee wall on the quay when I popped the question."

"What did ya say?"

"I asked her for a pair of her knickers. What the hell de ya think I said? I asked her would she be my wife."

"And the auld ejit said yes?"

"Yeah."

"When, when?"

"Jasus give us a chance. We have ta tell the parents yet so we have. Then we will organise a date. She wants to get married in April."

"Right, and where will ya live?"

"Don't know yet. I will have to start lookin' around for somewhere."

"There's a place ta rent up High Street."

"Know about that, might ask about it. Anyway, I have ta ask ya a question?"

"Yeah?"

"Will ya be my best man?"

"I would have punched ya on the nose if ya had asked anyone else."

"Great."

Later in the week, Po met Red in town and told him about his planned engagement party.

"Saturday night, now ya better be there, I'm warnin' ya," said Po pointing a finger at Red.

"Jasus, I'll be there for God's sake, who else will be there?"

"I've just asked a few of the lads, Jumpy and Dunno, Topcoat, Kitter, Shifty, The Bishop, Jammy and Anto."

"Right, I'll see ya there then."

"Ya better."

"I will, I will, ya nag."

Red arrived at McGee's lounge bar on the quay that Saturday night for Po and Trish's engagement party. The sound of music and noise bellowed through the open windows. As he entered he nodded a few hellos to people he knew before he found himself being grabbed by a small dark haired lady in her forties wearing a very bright floral dress.

"Come on handsome, let's dance."

Red was literally dragged onto the darkened dance floor to the sounds of 'Midnight' by the Shadows. He was held in a tight embrace by this lady whose hands were moving around his back.

"Ya have a nice body so ya have," she smiled up at him.

"Thanks," was all Red could manage to get out.

He felt her hands moving lower and lower. Soon they were on his backside.

"And a nice tight bum too."

Red just smiled, embarrassed. He was looking around for help, from anywhere, from anybody. It was not forthcoming. The hands were moving again. Her right hand moved across his hip and down to the front of his trousers where she began massaging gently.

"Hmm, you do have a nice body."

Just then the music stopped. Red looked down at the smiling lady.

"Thanks for the dance. Make sure ya keep me another one later. I have ta find some people, bye."

Red took off at speed. He found Po and Trish seated at a table in the corner.

"Jasus Po, ya have to help me out with a problem."

"What?"

"Don't let her see ya looking, but your one in the flowery dress over there?"

"Yeah, what about her?"

"She grabbed me by the balls on the dance floor so she did."

"She grabbed ya by . . . . ." Po was doubled.

Trish too was in fits of laughter.

"She pulled your willie . . . on the dance . . . floor?" roared Po.

"I'm glad ya find it so friggin' funny."

"Trish . . . tell . . . him."

"Red, that's my mom."

"What?"

"That's my mom."

Red put his face in his hands.

"Oh Jasus, frig me, oh shit."

"It's all right Red, mom gets a bit frisky when she has a few drinks."

"So did ya fancy her Red?" asked Po as he started roaring again with laughter. "She is a widow ya know . . . maybe ya could be my father in law," Po was enjoying himself.
"Piss off ya wee whorein' bastard."

Po and Trish had their engagement party, Anto and the boys all had a great time. Red had an unexpected erotic massage, which embarrassed him greatly, Po loved it.

Po said goodnight to Red at the front door of the pub. He was still laughing at Red's encounter with his future mother-in-law.
"I swear, I never thought in my lifetime I would ever see it," laughed Po.
"See what?"
"Red Morgan blushing because a woman was fondling his balls."

End

Po's Wedding

1974

Red opened his front door to find a smiling Po. He stood to one side to allow Po to come in. As he passed Red he got a slap on the back of the head.

"Hey, what was that for?" said Po, rubbing the back of his head.

"Nothin'. So, just wait till ya do somethin'."

"Got news."

"What?"

"Anyone in the kitchen?"

"Packed, why?"

"Let's go down the back yard."

"Ah. Secret, is it?" smiled Red, opening the back door.

Po didn't answer. They sat on a low wall that ran along Granddad Morgan's flower and vegetable garden.

"Well, what are ya bustin' ta tell me?"

"We picked the day."

"That's nice. What are ya goin' ta do with it?"

"Get married."

"What?"

"Get married."

"Get married? Yis have picked a day?"

"Yep. It will be on Saturday, 20th July."

"Jasus! That's only a couple a months away."

"Well, what do ya think?"

"Well, I suppose the date's ok, but it's just a couple of months away. Not a lot of time ta get organised."

"No problem. I have everything in hand."

"Bad habit, that."

This just got Red a punch on the arm.

"Stop messin', will ya? We have a load of things ta talk about."

"Like?"

"Ya'll have to know what ta do in the chapel with the ring and stuff. And ya'll have ta give a speech at the reception, and things like that."

"Jasus, forgot about the speech thing."

"Well, ya better get workin' on it."

"I'll just say ya are a wee whore and that poor girl doesn't know what she has let herself in for."

This just got Red another punch on the arm, harder this time.

"That was friggin' sore."

"It was meant ta be."

"Where are ya holdin' the reception?"

"In Magees."

"Good as anywhere, I suppose."

"Ya'll have ta go ta get measured for the dress suit."

"Hate them things."

"How could ya hate them things when ya never worn one before?"

"Well, everyone else says it, so I just thought I would."

"Well, it's the way Trish wants it."

"Well, ok. But, as long as it won't be like one of them American things."

"American things?"

"Yeah, ya know, sky blue suits."

"Jasus, no. Just normal black suits."

"Wow, this lot has given me somethin' ta think about, for sure. Where are yis goin' ta live?"

"We went ta see that house on High Street. It's grand and she liked it. It's even got hot water and a bathroom."

"Very up market."

"And the rent isn't too bad, either. I paid the deposit on it and got the key."

"And what about the honeymoon?"

"That's one of the things I wanted ta ask ya about. Where do ya think we should go?"

"Frig me Po, how the hell would I know? Take her ta Dublin."

"I was thinkin' that, my own self."

"There ya go, then."

∗   ∗   ∗

The two months passed, quickly. There was only one more important thing than the actual wedding to organise, according to Anto, and that was Po's 'Stag Night'.

Po was kept out of all the planning and was just told to be at Uncle Luigi's Café two nights before his wedding at 8.30pm. Trish warned Po that he was not to have a Stag Night, as per tradition, the night before his wedding. She, for some unknown reason, did not trust his friends to get him to the church.

One week before the Stag Night was to be held, a meeting was convened in Uncle Luigi's upstairs sitting room.

"Right. So are we agreed, then? We will hold it in the Waldorf lounge, ok?"

There followed a murmur of approval.

"And have we loads of nice things ready for wee Po?"

"Ohhh, yes," smiled Red.

"So what about wedding presents?" asked Bishop Keenan.

"I think my original idea is still the best," said Anto.

"Ok, tell us all again, Anto."

"Well, Po intends to just go ta Dublin and book into a Bed and Breakfast. He says they will stay for a week. Now, I have counted eleven of us that can get together and a few more we can approach. If we all buy presents he will end up with a load of useless stuff for sure."

"I was gettin' him a toaster. That's not useless," commented Jumpy.

"I was gettin' him a toaster, too," added Dunno.

"Jasus, see what a mean, Red?" put in Anto.

"Yeah, beginning to, all right," laughed Red.

"I think Anto has a good idea, there. If we all bunch together we can give them a honeymoon in London. I think they would prefer that ta havin' two toasters," said Bishop Keenan.

"I agree. Let's go with the honeymoon thing," said Ginger McVerry.

"Lets vote, then," said Anto. "All in favour of the honeymoon idea put up your hand."

All hands went up. So they decided on paying for Po and Trish's honeymoon.

"Red, you'll have ta make sure Po doesn't book anywhere in Dublin. Tell him he can just find a place when he gets there," said Anto.

"No problem," answered Red.

"Will we be able ta collect enough, between us, to cover everything?" asked Ginger.

"Good question. What do ya think, Anto?" asked Bishop.

"A think there will be, well enough. In fact, I think there will be money over. Don't forget, Uncle Luigi and our Roberto will be chippin' in."

"Will we just give them the money left over?" asked Jumpy.

"No, don't be silly, Jumpy. We are goin' ta book the Queen to meet them," sneered Red.

"Jasus, that'll be somethin'," put in Dunno.

"Oh, my God," said Anto, putting his face in his hands.

"Naw, Jumpy, a think the Queen might be a wee bit busy. So we'll just give them the money," said Red, seriously.

"Ah, right. Ok," replied Jumpy.

"So what about digs in London?" asked Bishop.

"I thought of that. A have a few relatives there, so I'll ring them and get them to organise that," said Anto.

*   *   *

Red called for Po, on the evening of his 'Stag Night'.

"Now, before we go down there, Morgan, a hope ya have no shit planned?"

"No, don't be silly."

"I know ya, Morgan. I wouldn't trust ya as far as a could throw an elephant."

"Meeee?"

"Yeah, you!"

"Jasus, as if a would. I don't believe in all that stuff."

"Of course, ya don't."

As Red and Po went through the doors of the Waldorf Lounge they were greeted with applause and cheering from over 20 waiting friends. Po bowed, with some style, and proceeded to take his seat at the table. Drinks appeared in front of him and Red.

Anto lifted his glass. "Can I be the first to make a toast, gentlemen?"

Everyone lifted their glasses.

"I know this is a happy time, but it is also a very sad one as well, We will be losin' a mate to the state of married life, where from Saturday, poor wee Po will need the wife's permission ta go ta football matches, ta meet his mates, and ta even go outta the house. The poor wee man will be nothin' short of a prisoner. So, friends, raise your glasses to Newry's very last over 12 year old, virgin."

"Here, here," was the unanimous reply, as they all sipped their drinks and applauded.

"Piss off, ya bunch of whores and fruits," replied Po, smiling.

"Now, as per tradition as ya all know, it is very bad luck for a bridegroom to be at his stag night wearin' his own clothes," said Boots Markey. Now, havin' that in mind, we brought along some clothes ta make him more comfortable."

This got a cheer from all there. Po was grabbed and quickly stripped to his underpants. He was then, in spite of a brave but losing struggle, dressed in a lovely spotted dress with a matching straw bonnet. His own clothes were quickly removed and hidden.

"Red, your turn for a toast," shouted Anto, over the general din.

Red stood up to the applause from all there.

"Now gentlemen, and of course those who are not sure, may I take this opportunity to wish my good friend, Po, a happy and joyous marriage. I know he will find it strange goin' ta bed with a woman for the first time, and havin' her see him without his wee teddy bear pyjamas."

This got a round of 'Oooos'.

"Therefore, may I present him with this small token of my appreciation on this great occasion?" Red handed Po a brown envelope. He opened it quickly and produced a small white handbook.

"Bastard," smiled Po.

He showed the book to all seated at the table.

'Sexual Intercourse for the First Time'.

This got a loud cheer.

"Raise your glasses, please, ta our wee Po and hope he can 'rise' to the occasion," said Red, loudly.

At the end of the night, Po was somewhat tipsy, but still aware of what was going on. He was unceremoniously grabbed and taken out of the pub onto Newry's Hill Street, where a small cart had mysteriously appeared. He was thrown into the cart, tied with a rope, and wheeled along the street to the singing sounds of his friends and the applause of bystanders. When the procession reached the top of the street, Po was taken from the cart, and dragged to one of Newry's landmarks, called, 'The Big Clock'. The clock, was about 20 feet tall, green, and situated in the middle of Margaret Square, at the top of Hill Street. He was tied to the bottom of the clock to loud applause and cheering.
Anto raised his arms to silence the crowd.
"Now gentlemen, please. Settle down. Settle down. To bring this night to a close, we are, of course, staying with tradition. We wish our friend, Po, all the happiness in the world. May his home never be without water, fruit, eggs and bread. To this end, would you all be kind enough to step forward and give to our friend a small token of these items."
Boxes of eggs and tomatoes, tins full of water, and bags full of flour appeared. The cheering began again, louder this time, as Po was pelted and drenched with all the materials provided.

*   *   *

The big day arrived, and everything that needed to be organised, was. Red was all dressed up in his Dress Suit, with bow tie, white rose in his lapel, and even shoes that had been shined, arrived at Po's house at 10.30 am. The wedding was to be at twelve mass in the Cathedral.

Po was a walking bundle of nerves, as he raced around, getting dressed.
"How are we for time, Red?" asked Po.
"We should have been there 10 minutes ago."
"Frig off, ya bastard."
"Ya have asked me that three times in this past ten minutes."
"So, I'm just a wee bit nervous ya know, so a am," complained Po.
"Ya have plenty of time, ya plank. The car is not pickin' ya up till a quarter past eleven. Can I ask somethin'?"

"What?"

"Your trousers?"

"What about them?"

"Why are ya holdin' them up?"

"Can't find the friggin' belt."

"Oh, I see. Can a ask another question?"

"What for frig sake?"

"Ya know the zipper?"

"What zipper?"

"The one ya pull your wee willie out of ta pee."

"What about it?"

"Should it not be in the front?"

Po looked down.

"Shit."

Red roared, laughing, as he fell back on Po's bed.

"All right for you, ya whore. Wait till it's your turn. We'll see what you're like."

Po's bedroom door opened and in came Anto.

"Anto, what are you doin' here?" asked Po, halfway into his trousers.

"Ah Jasus, Po, did a come at a bad time? I didn't mean ta interrupt yis."

"Would ya ever get stuffed, ya whore," snapped Po.

"Ya get everything organised, Anto?" asked Red.

"Yep, all organised."

"What are you two up ta?" asked Po.

"Have ya told Trish where yis are goin' for your honeymoon, yet?"

"No, a wanted ta surprise her. Why?"

Anto cleared his throat, "On behalf of all of us that do 'friend impersonations', includin' him, over there, and meself, I have been asked ta give ya this."

Anto handed Po a white envelope. He opened it and stared at Anto, then at Red, then back at Anto.

"These are tickets ta London," mumbled Po, quietly.

"Didn't a tell ya he wasn't slow, Anto?" smiled Red.

"I don't understand. They are for me?"

"For you and Trish. Yis are going ta London for your honeymoon. The digs and all that stuff have been organised. My cousin, Mario, will meet yis at the airport."

"Jasus."

"No. Mario," laughed Anto.

"Where did these come from?" asked Po.

"They're from all your mates and Uncle Luigi and Roberto," said Red.

"Frig me. A don't know what ta say."

"Now, there's history, Anto," said Red.

This got him a punch on the arm.

"This is brilliant! Friggin' London! Jasus!"

"Well, we thought ya would appreciate that more than toasters and dinner sets," said Red.

"And yis were right. This is the best present I could have got. It's just great! A would give yis a kiss except I know ya would only like it."

The limousine pulled up in front of the Cathedral. Po and Red got out and entered the church. There were quite a number of people already seated there, most of them recognised by Po, who smiled and nodded. He and Red reached the front of the church and took their places beside Po's mother, father, brother and sister.

"What if she doesn't turn up?" whispered Po to Red.

"She's not that bright, ya wally."

"Smart frigger."

Just then, the organ began playing. The congregation rose, the bride had arrived. Po and Red, both, looked towards the back of the church. Trish was already on her way to the altar, on the arm of her father. She looked radiant, glowing, and very beautiful.

"Jasus! She's gorgeous!" whispered Po.

"She looks like a movie star. Now I'm convinced ya must have drugged her," smiled Red.

This got him an elbow in the ribs.

Red and Po left their pew and took their place in front of the altar, to wait on Trish to arrive.

"Have ya the ring?" whispered Po.

"What ring?"

"The weddin' ring."

"Was I ta bring it?"

Po glared at him, colour leaving his face. Red smiled. Po seemed to start breathing, again.

"You're evil."

"Thanks."

When the ceremony was all over, and Po was now officially a member of the married community, the couple, followed by all the guests, made their way to the reception at Magees Public House. The pub looked fantastic, all decked out in ribbons and flowers and the tables beautifully laid out for the wedding dinner. When the meal was over, Red was told it was time for his Best Man duties to continue. He stood up and clinked his glass with a spoon to get attention. When the room went silent he began to speak.

"Holy Father, ladies and gentlemen. Thank you all for coming today, for this special occasion. I shall refer to the bridegroom, from here on in, as Po, which, is the name you all know him by. I could use some other names he is known by, but would not wish to embarrass this officious gathering. As you can see, I have no notes to read from. The speech Po gave me . . . . I have thrown away. Po is a wonderful guy. Honest, intelligent, giving, reliable, talented, caring and generous. Now, on the other hand, I am a liar who takes bribes to say nice things about people. I have known Po all my life. I even remember him sucking a 'dummy' in his pram. Actually, not many people know that he still sucks it when he thinks no one is watching. We went to Primary School together, as well as Secondary School. And we only parted when he went to Reform School. Seriously, ladies and gentlemen, we became friends more years ago than I can remember. We have played football together, played basketball together, gone to football matches all over Ireland and to England together. We worked together, here in Newry, and in Dublin. Though, in Dublin I did most of the work. One day, we were sitting, talking, and I remember asking him; 'Do ya think ya'll ever get married?' He replied, 'No'. I asked him why that was and he told me, 'The day will never come when I would be lucky enough to meet an angel' Ladies and gentlemen, he was wrong. He was lucky enough ta meet his angel. Will you be kind enough to raise your glasses to . . . . The Bride and Groom."

After the toast, Red received long and loud applause from all the guests, except Po, who stuck his tongue out.

The rest of the day went well. It was a happy and joyous occasion and all present had a great time. Po and Trish left early with Roberto, who was driving them to the airport.

Outside Magees, Po turned to Red and embraced him.

"Thanks for everything ya did."

"Sure, it was a pleasure. Have a good time."

"Don't worry. I will."

Po and Trish must have been hugged fifty times before she even got to throw her bouquet. It was caught by Red's girlfriend Maureen.

"You fixed that, ya wee runt."

Po just smiled and touched the side of his nose with his finger.

As the car began to move off, Po shouted to Red.

"But you're still a whore and a bastardin' fruit."

End